SPACE BAND

TOM FLETCHER

PUFFIN

PUFFIN BOOKS

UK | USA | Canada | Ireland | Australia
India | New Zealand | South Africa

Puffin Books is part of the Penguin Random House group of companies
whose addresses can be found at global.penguinrandomhouse.com

Penguin
Random House
UK

First published 2022
This edition published 2023

001

Text and illustrations copyright © Tom Fletcher, 2022
Interior illustrations and design by Dynamo
Cover illustrations by Shane Devries

Typeset in Baskerville MT Pro, Bad Medicine and Kabouter
Printed and bound in Great Britain by Clays Ltd, Elcograf S.p.A.

The authorized representative in the EEA is Penguin Random House Ireland,
Morrison Chambers, 32 Nassau Street, Dublin D02 YH68

A CIP catalogue record for this book is available from the British Library

ISBN: 978–0–241–59593–0

All correspondence to:
Puffin Books, Penguin Random House Children's
One Embassy Gardens, 8 Viaduct Gardens, London SW11 7BW

For all the

GALAXY DEFENDERS

Welcome to

SPACE BAND

Superfans have recorded their
own versions of The Earthlings' songs!

As you read the story,
look out for this symbol:

It tells you that the song is available online.
Just scan this QR code to listen!

https://linktr.ee/spacebandalbum
This will take you to another website,
so please ask a grown-up.

MEET THE BAND!

GEORGE

Bass-player, lead singer, and founder of **THE EARTHLINGS**. George is the universe's biggest fan of Max Riff and the Comets!

NEILA

Guitarist, broccoli fan, and the smartest kid at school – though she's a little stage-shy. You'll never see Neila without her **LUCKY HAT!**

BASH

Drummer and **SPACE SUPERFAN**. Bash always carries spare drumsticks and a copy of his favourite magazine: *WE ARE NOT ALONE!*

CONTENTS

INTRO

I'm **GEORGE**.
George Racket.
I play **BASS GUITAR**.

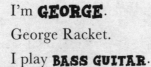

And this is **NEILA**.
She plays **GUITAR**.

This is **BASH**.
He plays the **DRUMS**.

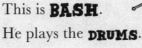

1

And together we are . . .

THE EARTHLINGS!

The best band
in the universe!

We never meant to become intergalactic rock stars, or to save the world from being pulverized by evil aliens using only the power of music. It just sort of . . . happened.

We weren't always super-awesome, guitar-shredding, drum-soloing music legends either.

In fact, before we were unexpectedly beamed up into outer space, we were actually pretty awful. And I don't mean just a bad band.

We TOTALLY SUCKED!

I'm serious. Our own parents couldn't even pretend to like the noises that leaked out of our garage – the place where we rehearsed every day after school. And parents are supposed to like *everything* their kids do!

We were so bad that our neighbours moved house. And our neighbours' neighbours. And even their neighbours too!

I bet you're thinking, *How did the worst band in the world become the best band in the universe?*

I guess it all began on the day I started writing my own songs and decided to put them all down in a book.

This book, in fact. The book you're about to read.

So turn the volume up to infinity, and get ready to rock 'n' roll out of this solar system.

It's time for lift-off!

TRACK 1

THE BOOK OF ROCK

NAME: GEORGE RACKET

SUBJECT: ~~Science~~ ROCK 'N' ROLL

TEACHER: ~~Mr Lloyd~~ LIFE!

Welcome to the book that's going to change my life.

That's right. This is **THE** book. The book that's going to turn me, George Racket, from the ordinary, slightly-shorter-than-average ten-year-old into a super-awesome international

ROCK STAR!

OK, I know on the outside this book looks like a normal school exercise book . . . and it kind of is. (I 'borrowed' it from the classroom supply cupboard.) But that's just a clever disguise.

It will be on these very pages, where boring equations and snore-fest theories would normally be written, that I shall write my masterpiece of musical awesomeness!

Normal exercise book

THIS – my first-ever *songbook*!

No, hang on. *Songbook* sounds a bit rubbish.

My first-ever *music book*?

Nope.

Wait. I've got it . . .

MY BOOK OF ROCK!

To be honest, I'm not quite sure how to write songs yet, but my music idol, rock-legend Max Riff, lead singer of the Comets, once said:

> THE GREATEST SONGS ARE BASED ON REAL EXPERIENCES, DUDE. LIVE. WRITE. ROCK!

Live. Write. Rock! If that worked for Max Riff, it can work for George Racket! So I've decided I should start writing down everything that happens to me.

That's right. **EVERYTHING**.

Starting now!

OK, let's see . . . I'm in the most **BORING** lesson at Greyville School: Mr Lloyd's science class. He's got his usual white lab coat on and his hair looks like a science experiment itself.

I don't think he really needs to wear a lab coat in class. It'd be a bit like our history teacher, Mr Bygone, dressing like Henry VIII. Or our maths teacher, Mrs Spearing, dressing like a calculator. Or Ms Feather, our art teacher, dressing like a pencil.

Mr Lloyd is writing something on the board. Something about space – but no one is listening, because there's something **WAY** more interesting going on.

There's a **PIGEON** on the windowsill. An actual pigeon. Just staring right at Danika Chowdhury.

No, wait . . .

It just flew away.

It's flying over the car park and . . . ew, gross! It just did its business on Mr Lloyd's car!

Oooh, this **HAS** to be turned into a song . . .

PIGEON

by George Racket

Fly away, pigeon.
Coo, coo, coo . . .
Is it gonna fly over
You-ooh-ooh?
Flyin' is what pigeons
Do, do, do . . .
I think I just saw it do a
Doo-doo!

Doo-doo-doo!
I think I just saw it do a
Doo-doo-doo!
I think a pigeon did a
Doo-doo-doo!
Cos every pigeon loves a
Doo-doo-doo!
Doo-doo, doo-doo
ON YOU!

Whoop! That's one song in my book of rock! Strong start. The bar has been set high. This is going well, right? We'll have an album in no time.

What else is happening? Oh, it's starting to rain, which probably means we'll all have to stay inside at lunch.

RUBBISH!

Don't get me wrong. I love staying inside at lunch. That's what I always try to do! While everyone else rushes outside to play footie or dodgeball, I get the *music room* all to myself for an hour and can shred some sick riffs on the school guitar, in between eating my cheese-and-Marmite sandwich.

OK, so it's not the best guitar in the world, but any guitar is better than no guitar! I'd way rather stay inside and play that plank of wood with strings than be

picked **LAST** for the football team again, or get whacked in the face with a cold dodgeball!

But on wet days *everyone* has to stay inside, and I can forget all about getting the music room to myself. Most of the other kids muck about with the instruments as though they're just toys. Last week, Dylan Bodkins was using the guitar like a bow and arrow, pulling back the strings to fire drumsticks across the room.

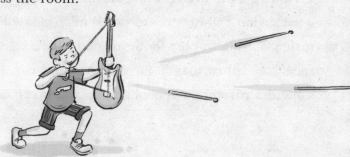

Let me tell you something right now. A guitar is **NOT** a toy. It is a precious, finely crafted tool used by the most fearless warriors alive – *musicians*!

OK, let's see. What else can I write about in my book of rock? The science room smells a bit funny, like vinegar, but not the good kind of vinegar that you put on battered sausage and chips from Fred's, my favourite chippy (oooh, think I might have that for dinner tonight!). It's more like the kind of vinegary liquid that scientists use to pickle gross things in jars.

Some people reckon Mr Lloyd has got a jar of real human eyeballs in the store cupboard and that's where the smell comes from.

Hmmm.

Wait, what rhymes with **'SAUSAGE'**?

Porridge?

Orange?

Squash-it?

Nothing rhymes with 'sausage'! Not sure if this story is going to make a good song, but it's worth a try . . .

~~PICKLED EYES~~ NOTHING RHYMES WITH 'SAUSAGE'!

by George Racket

Eyes in the dark
Looking for the light,
Smelling kind of funny,
Giving me a fright.
Vinegar is great
When it's on a sausage,
But in a jar of eyes . . .

Nothing rhymes with 'sausage'!
Nothing rhymes with 'sausage'!
Nothing rhymes with 'sausage'!
Nothing rhymes with 'sausage'!
Nothing rhymes with it.

Eyes in a jar
Make me feel sick.
Looking through the glass -
Bring a bucket quick!

Wish I didn't eat
The chips and battered sausage.
It tasted really good but . . .

Nothing rhymes with 'sausage'!
Nothing rhymes with 'sausage'!
Nothing rhymes with 'sausage'!
Nothing rhymes with 'sausage'!
Nothing rhymes with 'sausage'.

NO WAY!
What about 'orange'?
NO WAY!
Does it rhyme with 'porridge'?
NO WAY!

Could it rhyme with 'storage'?
NO WAY!

Nothing rhymes with 'sausage'!
Nothing rhymes with 'sausage'!
Nothing rhymes with 'sausage'!

Nothing rhymes with 'sausage'!
Nothing rhymes with it.

I don't think it'll make the album, but it just goes to show that Max Riff was right. You can write a song about *anything*. If I keep writing it all down – the good, the bad and the vinegary – soon I'll have a book of songs that will rock the socks off the whole world!

Oooh, now *that* sounds like a song too . . .

ROCK THE SOCKS OFF THE WORLD

by George Racket

A rock song don't have
   to make any sense
To understand it.
The world don't have
   to wear any socks
Cos it's a planet.

But if it did wear socks I think that
They would be big ones!
(Really big ones!)

From the ground up to the sky
And that's why . . .

We're gonna rock, let's rock, let's rock the socks,
Rock the socks off the world!
Let's rock, let's rock, let's rock the socks
Off all the boys and the girls!

Rock the socks off your mum and dad
And all your brothers and sisters!
Gonna rock those socks so bad
You're gonna get rock-and-roll blisters!

Let's rock, let's rock, let's rock the socks,
Rock the socks, rock the socks off the world!
(He's rocking them off!)
Rock the socks, rock the socks off the world!
(He's rocking them off!)
Rock the socks, rock the socks off the world!

Wow! Those lyrics just flew into my head out of nowhere, like I *had* to write them down. I think Max Riff calls it *inspiration* . . . or maybe it's *perspiration*. I can't remember. It's definitely *something*-spiration, anyway. I suppose that might start happening all the time now that I'm writing my life down in search for songs for my band.

OH YEAH! I didn't even finish telling you about my band!

I guess I should write a little introduction about who we are.

This calls for a new page.

TRACK 2

THE EARTHLINGS

That's our band name. The Earthlings.

And here's our logo (designed by me):

There are three of us in the band. Me, Bash and Neila. First up, on the drums, we have Bash.

Bash isn't his real name. His real name is Bari Bashar. Why do we call him Bash? Well, he just really liked *bashing* things

when he was little. So much so that 'bash' was actually his first word!

So his mum started calling him Bash and the name stuck like gum on a shoe, and he's been called Bash ever since.

One day, Bash's mum and dad had enough of all their nice things getting smashed by Bash, and they bought him a drum kit.

Well, that was a game changer. Finally, he had something that he was *allowed* to bash! Something to focus all his best bashing energy on!

The funny thing is he's not really that into music. Sure, Bash loves banging out a rock song because he gets to hit things and make loud noises without being told off – but what Bash is *really* into is **SPACE**.

If I'm a music nerd, then he's a total space geek!

It all started about a year ago when he thought he saw a UFO crash in the woods, through his bedroom window. **(I KNOW!)** Ever since then, Bash has been **OBSESSED** with space and science fiction and totally ridiculous, unrealistic stories about aliens destroying Earth, which explains some of the band-name suggestions that he submitted for consideration.

Then one day he insisted we watch this old black-and-white sci-fi movie about a bunch of really fake-looking aliens who beamed up a load of people from Earth and called them *earthlings*.

'That's it!' Bash cheered.

'What's *it*?' I said.

'Our band name. I've got it. What planet do we come from?'

'Well, I'm from Earth. I'm not sure about you, though,' I replied.

'Right! We're from Earth, so we are . . .'

I blinked back at him without the foggiest idea what he meant.

'We are Earthlings! *That's* our band name: **THE EARTHLINGS!**' he said triumphantly.

Well, after reading his list of other suggestions (including the Gassy Giants and Hubble Trouble) I figured The Earthlings was the best of a bad bunch. I won't lie – I didn't really like it at first, but Bash said, 'I'm only going to play drums in this band if I get to name it!' and we *really* needed a drummer, so I had no choice.

From then on, Bash was in the band and we were officially called The Earthlings!

Now he never leaves the house without a pair of drumsticks in his hands, plus a few spare pairs in his trusty backpack (just in case he rocks too hard and breaks one), along with a bunch of dorky space magazines.

Right, that's enough about him. Next is our face-melting, riff-shredding, eardrum-popping lead guitarist: Neila!

Neila is an onion.

Not literally, obviously. That'd just be weird. What I mean is that Neila's . . . complicated. She's surprising. Like a planet, she's got layers.

The first thing you see when you look at Neila is her 'lucky hat', which she **NEVER** takes off. Under that is a puff of fringe that always gets in her eyes. That's the crust.

Then comes the mantle, when you get to know her a little better. That's when you find out that she loves broccoli, but she doesn't like chocolate. Not even my favourite chocolate-covered peanut-butter cups!

(I KNOW!)

Then, when you get to the outer core, you discover that Neila is super smart. Seriously. She's full of nerdy knowledge that she'll probably never use, like the seven times table and what S is on the periodic table. (It's sulphur, by the way – the stuff that makes that bum gas smell!)

But underneath all those layers Neila's inner core is made of pure rock 'n' roll.

The only problem is that she's just a little scared to let it out. (The rock 'n' roll, not the bum gas.)

Neila only started at Greyville School a year ago after moving here from another town. It's always hard starting a new school and making new friends, but Neila didn't help herself. For example, she always sat **RIGHT** at the front of every class. In fact, she's still sitting there at this very moment! Right under Mr Lloyd's hairy nose! There's no way I'd get away with writing my book of rock if I was sitting next to Neila in the front row.

The front row is for kids who are going places. One place in particular: the prize-giving ceremony at the end of term, where all the parents get invited and Ms Feather gets too emotional and cries. Neila is definitely a prize-winning kind of kid, and I'm definitely not, so we weren't always the **BFFS** we are today.

But that all changed one lunch break a couple of months ago. I was heading for the usually empty music room, but as I got closer to the door I could hear there was already someone inside.

Someone playing the most earth-shattering riffs I'd ever heard!

I **HAD** to find out who it was. So I did the obvious thing. I hid.

My cover was blown when the bell rang for the end of lunch, and I saw Neila sneaking out of the room and back to class. I was so stunned that I fell into the fire extinguisher.

So that's Bash and Neila, which just leaves **ME**.

I play the bass guitar. 'Bass' rhymes with 'ace' or 'race', not 'pass' or 'class' – just in case you're wondering! The bass is like a normal guitar, except it only has four strings and the sound it makes is super low. I decided to become a bass player because I thought learning four strings would be easier than six, but I was **WAY** wrong. The four bass strings are like thick, metal worms, and when I first started to play, my fingers went all blistered and looked super gross!

I almost gave up, but then I remembered what Max Riff once said . . .

> ## IF YOU NEVER GIVE UP ON MUSIC, MUSIC WILL NEVER GIVE UP ON YOU.

So I didn't give up on music. I stuck with it. And one day I woke up and found that the ends of my fingers had gone hard . . . **ROCK** hard! Like those fake plastic thumbs you get at the magic shop.

'They're called calluses,' Mum explained when I ran downstairs to show her.

I like to call them my **ROCK FINGERS!**

From then on, I could rock out as hard as I wanted without my fingers feeling as if they were on fire. The only downside is that I can't really feel anything with the tips of my fingers any more. Seriously, I think they're pretty much indestructible.

My bass guitar is my **FAVOURITE** thing in the whole universe. It was my birthday present last year, and I still can't believe it's mine. It's a Fender P. Bass (the P stands for Precision, which my dad says is ironic when I play it, whatever that means) and the colour is cosmic green. I think it's called that because it has all these little sparkly bits in the paint that catch the light like stars and look SO awesome.

I wanted to get cosmic-green glasses to match, but Mum said, 'Sparkly green glasses are not appropriate for school!'

(I KNOW!)

To top off the killer paint job, I've paired it with a black strap that has a white lightning bolt zapping down the front, like it's being struck with a thousand volts of pure electricity.

POW!

It's just like the one that Max Riff used to play before he SMASHED it up at the end of a legendary concert. It broke into a thousand pieces and looked like an explosion of stardust. I've got a poster of the moment he did it on my bedroom wall.

Smashing your guitar is probably the most rock 'n' roll thing anyone could ever do, but there's no way I'd ever do that to my Cosmo. Not in a million light years!

Oh yeah, that's my guitar's name – **COSMO.**

And don't even get me started on the sound. It's like a cross between a sports car revving its engine and a rocket launching into space – deep and growly. Well, that's what it's *supposed* to sound like, but I've only been playing it for a few months, so sometimes it sounds a bit . . . flappy. Bash says it's a bit like an elephant's bum after it's been eating baked beans. But I'll keep practising.

I'll never give up on music.

Anyway, that's my band! The Earthlings had assembled, and were ready to rock the stage. Although technically we've not rocked out on an actual stage yet. Just my parents' garage. But that's all about to change – TOMORROW – when we enter **GREYVILLE SCHOOL'S BATTLE OF THE BANDS.**

It's going to be our first-EVER show in front of a real live audience! It's a little terrifying, but totally worth it, because the first prize is . . .

Tickets to see **MAX RIFF AND THE COMETS** on Saturday night!

That's right. Max Riff and the Comets are in town for one night only, this Saturday! The tickets sold out in a record-breaking three seconds, so this is our only shot at being at that show.

To be honest, though, I don't think we stand much chance of winning. I mean, all the other bands are **WAY** older than us and have been playing for much longer. Plus, when we were rehearsing in the garage this week, Dad said we sounded like a car crash. (Seriously, he actually thought a car had crashed into the garage and called the police.)

So I guess that means we're probably not the best band in the world (yet). Still, I bet we're not the worst! There's got to be a band on the planet that sucks more than us . . . right?

OK, Mr Lloyd is making us copy something down from the board. I'd better do it or I'll get in trouble. Don't worry, though, there are more songs to come after this short break for some science!

TRACK 3

THE MINERVA 7

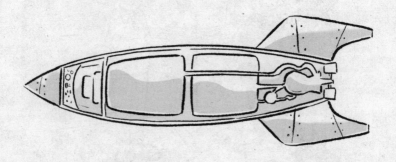

In 1985, a unique rocket was launched into space from Earth, carrying on board some of the most precious cargo known to mankind. As well as a number of top-secret scientific experiments . . . blah, blah, blah . . .

Science lessons can be **S00000000** boring and **S000000** long. If this lesson was a song, it would be the longest song ever!

Wait – that's given me an idea for a song!

THE LONGEST SONG EVER

by George Racket

It's the longest song,
It goes on and on . . .
You can sing this song forever! (Forever!)
The longest song,
It goes on and on . . .
When will this song end? NEVER!

CHORUS
The longest, longest, longest song,
The longest, longest song! (So long!)
The longest, longest, longest song,
This is the longest song . . .

REPEAT VERSE AND CHORUS

REFRAIN
On and on, it goes on and on . . .
Goes on and on!
It goes on and on! . . .

REPEAT ENTIRE SONG FOREVER . . .

This whole lesson is useless to me anyway. I'm going to be a rock star! I'm never going to need to know anything about space!

Bash is sitting a few seats away from me, and he could not look more excited. I don't know why he finds it all so fascinating. It's all *quantum this, light-year that*.

Although . . .

I can't believe I'm saying this, but it turns out there *is* something pretty cool about the *Minerva 7*!

Listen to this.

According to Mr Lloyd, the rocket's main 'mission objective' was to carry a satellite into orbit that would then zoom off into deep space. OK, so that might not sound too exciting, but get this: on board that satellite was **MUSIC!**

And it was every type of music you can imagine: from classical to hip-hop, opera to blues, reggae to rap, pop to punk. It was a musical snapshot of life on Planet Earth. NASA – that's the National Aeronautics and Space Administration in America, the space super-nerds who are in charge of sending rockets up into the cosmos – hoped that one day, aliens **(I KNOW!)** might discover it.

But here's where it gets **SUPER AWESOME**. NASA also had a brand-new, top-secret song written specially for the mission.

'NASA wanted a song that would give any alien life out there an idea of what it means to live on this planet. So they called upon a popular music group of the time,' Mr Lloyd said, cleaning his glasses.

'A "music group"? Do you mean a band?' asked Neila.

'Yes, yes, a band,' he confirmed.

My ears pricked up. A band . . . music . . . this science class was getting interesting all of a sudden.

'Mr Lloyd, what band?' I asked.

Mr Lloyd paused for a moment and looked at me,

frowning slightly. I could understand why he was confused. This was the first time I'd ever asked a question in his class.

'Oh, they were from the eighties, George. Long before you lot were born. I doubt any of you've heard of them,' Mr Lloyd said.

'Try me,' I said. I might not have been around in the eighties – even my mum and dad were only just around in the eighties! – but when it comes to music, that's my era!

'Well, funnily enough, the band has a space-themed name too. Perhaps that's one of the reasons NASA picked them. The lead singer was called Max R–'

'MAX RIFF?' I yelled.

Mr Lloyd looked at me in astonishment. 'Yes! Max Riff and the Comets. You've heard of them?'

Dylan Bodkins laughed. 'Of course we've heard of Max Riff and the Comets! Who hasn't?'

'They're total legends, sir!' Danika added, pointing to a Max Riff badge pinned to her school bag (next to a cool shiny red one).

'Well, I've never really understood the point of music, but I suppose they do have the odd catchy tune or two,' Mr Lloyd said.

'Yeah, they're only like

THE GREATEST BAND ON THE PLANET, Mr Lloyd!' Bash said.

'And OFF the planet too!' Neila added, pointing to the diagram of the *Minerva 7* on the board.

'So you're telling me that there's a Max Riff and the Comets song that I've never heard?' I had to double-check.

'Correct, George. In fact, no one on Earth has ever heard it! It was written and recorded in top secret in a state-of-the-art recording facility, deep underground at NASA,' Mr Lloyd explained with a twinkle in his eye. 'Then the song was loaded into the satellite and straight on to the *Minerva 7*, ready to be launched into space so that one day it might be discovered by extraterrestrial life.'

I felt my mouth drop open. Well, my mind was **BLOWN**. Science just got a whole lot more awesome!

Bash was grinning at me. It was a bit like he was saying, **'SEE? I TOLD YOU SO!'**

And, I had to admit, I *almost* wanted to rethink my whole future career choice from rock star to astronaut, just so I could go out and listen to that Max Riff song for myself.

'But why did no one from Earth ever get to listen to it?' I asked.

'Ah, that's the most fascinating part of this story!' Mr Lloyd said excitedly. 'Once the *Minerva 7* arrived at its destination, the secret new song was going to be transmitted down to Earth – all the way from space! But NASA lost contact with the *Minerva 7* shortly after it left the Earth's atmosphere. And to this day no one knows what happened to it.'

I felt my mouth drop open again.

'THEY LOST IT?'

Yeah, that's right. They lost a giant space rocket! Mr Lloyd explained that one minute it was there, a little **BLIP – BLIP – BLIP** on the radar, heading out into the solar system, then . . .

GONE!

Pretty careless, if you ask me. I mean, rockets are **MASSIVE**, aren't they? Imagine being the scientist in charge of a huge, whopping great gravity-defying rocket ship, then losing it the second it reaches space!

But, if losing a multi-million-dollar space rocket wasn't bad enough, the real tragedy is the unheard Max Riff and the Comets song that was lost with it!

Hang on . . .

Mr Lloyd just hit us with some more knowledge that puts an extra twist on this mysterious disappearing rocket:

'The *Minerva 7* wasn't just carrying a satellite full

of music. There was something else on board. Or . . . *someone*.'

OK, Mr Lloyd is now doing the thing where he doesn't tell us the answer until after break. He likes leaving us on a cliffhanger so that we actually *want* to come back to class and find out what happens. This might work on Bash every time, but it has never once worked on me before – until today! I want to know who was on that rocket!

Can you imagine being on a space rocket, then losing communication with ground control and drifting off into space? A total loner in the universe, with no one to bother you and nothing to keep you company but an endless supply of the world's greatest music . . .

THAT SOUNDS AWESOME!

LONER

by George Racket

It's quiet in the universe.
No chorus, middle eight or verse.
And things are only getting worse.
I'm alone, I'm alone,
So alone . . .

It's silent in the Milky Way.
E.T. isn't on his way.
No one's coming out to play.
I'm alone, so alone . . .
I'm the loner of the universe.

CHORUS
Turn the radio up on this rocket.
No one else around can stop it.
Not a soul is passing me by.
I'm a shooting star in the sky,
A million miles away from home

Halfway across the universe . . .
And I'm alone.

I travelled into outer space,
I haven't seen a friendly face.
I guess I'm an acquired taste.
I'm alone, so alone . . .
I'm the loner of the universe.

CHORUS

On my own, I'm on my own . . .
I'm alone - yeah, I'm alone!
On my own, I'm on my own . . .
I'm alone - yeah, I'm alone!
On my own, I'm on my own . . .
I'm alone - yeah, I'm alone!

It's quiet in the universe.
One small step and I'm the first
To sing a chorus, middle eight and verse.
I'm alone, so alone,
I'm alone . . .

CHORUS

TRACK 4

DISASTER AT BREAKTIME!

It was the dreaded *wet breaktime* I'd feared, and I'd raced to the music room as soon as I'd finished scribbling down the lyrics to 'Loner'. Neila and Bash were waiting for me. Unfortunately, about half the school was there too.

We found a quiet corner and I showed them my new song.

'A song about space! Yeah!' cried Bash happily. (Phew!)

'Those lyrics are **AWESOME**, George,' Neila said (double phew!), then she picked up the school guitar to start figuring out the chords. 'And there's a solo for me!'

Here's where it all went wrong.

Just as I finished reading the last chorus, I realized that *someone* was standing close by, earwigging in on our conversation, and that someone was **ALFIE BIFFSON!**

Alfie Biffson is in Year Six and has a band too. They're called the **BONEHEADZ**, and I used to think they were the most super-awesome band in the whole world (apart from Max Riff and the Comets, obviously). Before I had my own band, I would secretly watch the Boneheadz rehearse in the music room and wish that I could be in their band.

I even thought that wish might come true once. Their bass player left Greyville to go to boarding

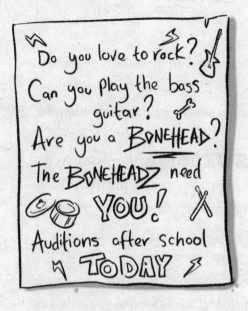

Do you love to rock?
Can you play the bass guitar?
Are you a BONEHEAD?
The BONEHEADZ need
YOU!
Auditions after school
TODAY

school, and the Boneheadz were holding auditions for a replacement!

I went to the audition ready to show them what I could do, but when I got there everyone else was at least a year older and a foot taller than me.

'Hi, I'm here to be your new bass player!' I said with what I thought was the perfect balance of politeness and confidence.

Alfie took one look at me and burst out laughing.

'The guitar is bigger than he is!' he howled, and all the other Boneheadz started laughing too.

'This isn't a *baby* band.'

'The nursery auditions are tomorrow!'

'Can ickle bassy-wassy boy sing his alphabet?'

Needless to say, I didn't get into the band.

That was the day I stopped listening to the Boneheadz. Unfortunately, everyone else at school thinks the Boneheadz are the best thing since sliced bread, and all because they won Greyville School's Battle of the Bands last year. But that's probably because . . .

Oh, yeah. That's the other reason I'm not sure we're in with much chance of winning this contest. Probably the biggest reason. The head judge!

The head judge is our music teacher. And our music teacher is . . . drum roll, please . . .

MR BIFFSON. Also known as Alfie's dad!

(I KNOW!)

For the past year, Alfie has walked around like he thinks he's a true rock star, with slicked-back hair that always looks as if he's just got out of the shower. I don't know about you, but when I get out of the shower my mum makes me dry my hair properly.

So anyway . . .

'Nice little poem you've written there, *Specs*!' Alfie scoffed at me while putting his fingers round his eyes, pretending they were glasses. *Hilarious.*

'It's not a *poem*, it's a **SONG**,' I snapped back at him.

Silence fell around us as if someone had just vacuumed up the sound in the music room with a giant Henry Hoover!

Alfie's Boneheadz bandmates suddenly appeared out of nowhere, all sporting the exact same slicked-back, sticky-looking haircut, as if someone had dropped a tub of hair gel into a cloning machine.

'Oh, so the baby bass player is a baby *songwriter* now too?' Alfie said with a fake impressed expression on his face.

'Yeah, and we're going to win this year's Battle of the Bands!' Bash said, appearing by my side.

There was a moment of silence, then all the Boneheadz burst into uncontrollable laughter.

'You? Win the Battle of the Bands?'

'Make sure your mummy changes your nappy before you play!'

Neila hid her face behind her long, curly jet-black fringe as if she was closing the curtains on the world, and slid behind me.

Alfie called for his Boneheadz to be quiet and said, 'Well, go on, then.'

'Go on what?' I asked.

'Sing us one of your *amazing* songs.'

My heart felt like Bash was playing a drum solo in my chest. The thought of performing in front of *actual* people was . . .

AWESOME!

This could be our FIRST-EVER GIG outside my parents' garage! The moment we'd been waiting for!

Were we ready? Nope!

Would we suck? Maybe.

Was I going to miss a chance to rock out in front of an actual crowd? **NO WAY!**

'All right. I will,' I said, face to face with Alfie (well, it was more my face to his chest), lead singer to lead singer.

Bash grabbed a tambourine from the box of percussion instruments and gave us a nod. *Ready!*

'Neila, are you ready to play?' I whispered, turning round this very book of rock so we could all see the chords to 'Loner' scribbled on the page.

Neila looked down. 'I . . . I . . . I don't know if I can.'

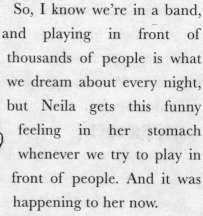

So, I know we're in a band, and playing in front of thousands of people is what we dream about every night, but Neila gets this funny feeling in her stomach whenever we try to play in front of people. And it was happening to her now.

'It's like I've been zapped with a freeze ray!' she hissed through clenched teeth.

I've looked it up before, and it's called *stage fright*, which I think is a silly name for it. She's not scared of the stage. It's the audience watching her that she finds scary. It should be called *audience fright*.

'Come on, Neila! I know you can do it!' I whispered, and Bash nodded.

As she nervously pulled the frayed strap of the school guitar over her head with trembling hands, I could sense the weight of the splintered wood weighing down on her shoulders.

'What's the matter? Aren't you going to play the song?' scoffed Alfie.

Neila just stared at the guitar as though she was desperately trying to play it with the power of her mind.

'You *can* do this, Neila! Think of it like a warm-up for the Battle of the Bands!' Bash said.

'Yeah, show them how awesome you are!' I whispered.

The kids around us were starting to whisper and giggle as Neila placed her fingers on the tired strings and gave me a tiny, terrified nod.

READY!

I closed my eyes, took a breath and counted us in.
'One! Two! Three –'

RIIIIIIIIIIIIIING!

The school bell blasted around the room. Break was over.

'Saved by the bell,' Alfie scorned. 'We'll see you at the battle.'

'Yeah. May the best band win!' I called after him as he and his Boneheadz left the room, and we all headed back to class in silence.

TRACK 5

ARMSTRONG

Neila could barely look at me and Bash as we walked back into Mr Lloyd's classroom.

'It's OK! We'll head straight to the garage and practise again after school and –' I started to call over to her, but then Mr Lloyd clapped his hands for quiet.

In all the drama of wet break, I'd almost forgotten the cliffhanger he'd left us on: the mystery of the *someone* who was on board the *Minerva 7* when it disappeared. It turned out to be the saddest part of this space story, and Mr Lloyd dropped it on us with no warning.

Get your tissues ready.

I now know who my song 'Loner' is about, because there was indeed an astronaut on board the *Minerva 7*.

Not a *human* astronaut.

A CHIMP.

Armstrong the Astro-Ape.

Mr Lloyd put a photo of him on the board that was taken just before launch. Here's my copy of it:

Poor little guy.

'Mr Lloyd, why was a chimp allowed on to a spacecraft in the first place?' asked Bash.

Mr Lloyd nodded. 'Good question. Armstrong was on board as an experiment. NASA wanted to test whether chimpanzee astronauts could perform simple space tasks. Armstrong's mission was to press a button once the rocket had reached orbit that would safely release the payload –'

'You mean the satellite containing all the awesome Earth music and stuff?'

'Yes, George, the satellite containing "all the

awesome Earth music and stuff",' said Mr Lloyd, smiling. 'Then the *Minerva 7* would return little Armstrong back to Earth.

'Unfortunately, as we found out before break, that never happened. The rocket vanished, along with everything on board – including little Armstrong the Astro-Ape.'

The whole class was pretty quiet for the rest of Mr Lloyd's lesson. I could tell we were all thinking about Armstrong. I wonder what happened to him and that rocket full of awesome music. Mr Lloyd explained that some people believe that the ship broke apart in the upper atmosphere. Others think it could have drifted into deep space.

Whatever happened, it must have been **TERRIFYING**.

Who knows? Maybe little Armstrong managed to unbuckle his harness, climb out of his seat, take the controls to the rocket, crank up the volume on some of that Earth music on board, and speed off across the Milky Way on his own space adventure. Maybe even to discover his own planet!

Yeah. I'm just going to tell myself that's what happened.

I think I've come up with another song . . .

PLANET OF THE APES
by George Racket

Ooh-ooh, aah-aah! Ooh-ooh, aah-aah!
Ooh-ooh, aah-aah! Ooh-ooh, aah-aah!

Ch-ch-ch-chimp, chimp, chimp in outer space
Said goodbye to the human race.
The first on Earth to ever escape,
To find his very own personal p-p-p-planet of the
apes.

Aah-aah! Ooh-ooh, aah-aah! Ooh-ooh!

Ch-ch-ch-chimp, chimp in a rocket ship.
The first primate on an interstellar trip,
Having a blast eating bananas and grapes
On his very own personal p-p-p-planet of the apes.

Aah-aah! Ooh-ooh, aah-aah! Ooh-ooh!

He won't send a letter home
Because he don't know how to write.
He was only trained to fly a million-dollar rocket
Into suborbital space flight!

Ch-ch-ch-chimp, chimp, chimp among the stars.
He's not going to land on Jupiter or Mars.
Got coordinates set for just one place.
It's his very own personal p-p-p-planet of the apes.

Aah-aah! Ooh-ooh, aah-aah!
Ooh-ooh, aah-aah! Ooh-ooh, aah-aah . . .

TRACK 6

BAND BATTLE PRACTICE

It's not very rock 'n' roll in our garage, but once you get used to the smell . . . and the dust . . . and the mouse that lives in the wall . . . it's actually pretty cool.

I found an old Polaroid camera and a bunch of film in a box when we were rearranging our equipment, so I'm using it to take some behind-the-scenes pics of our journey to being rock stars.

Mum let us hang the Christmas lights in the garage so it kind of looks like a stage (if you squint your eyes), and when my parents aren't 'keeping an eye on us' (spying on us) we like using Dad's **SUPER-BEAM 900** torch as a spotlight.

Bash reckons it can be seen from space. I've told him that's totally ridiculous, but it still doesn't stop Bash lying in the garden after band practice, flashing Morse code at the sky.

Neila was THIRTY minutes late for band practice tonight. On one hand, that's pretty rock 'n' roll – I mean, no rock star is meant to show up on time – but, on the other hand, it meant I had to sit and listen to Bash bang on about the latest issue of his favourite space magazine, *We Are Not Alone.*

'Sorry, Bash, but we are totally alone. There's no such thing as aliens,' I told him for the

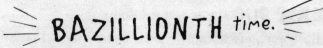 **BAZILLIONTH** time.

'Of course there is!' he said matter-of-factly. 'Even NASA must think so, right? Why else would they send the *Minerva 7* to space full of music for aliens to discover? And, anyway, how else do you explain crop circles or the sightings of mysterious lights in the sky all around the world?'

'I dunno, could be anything. Farmers having a laugh? Pilots getting lost? There's loads of explanations more believable than little green men in flying saucers whizzing across the sky!' I laughed. 'Listen, if you want to sleep over tonight, you can't talk to me about space all night.' I paused. 'Actually, you can. It'll help me get to sleep!'

Bash pulled a face at me. 'Hey, here's Neila!'

'Sorry, guys!' called Neila as her bike swung into the garage. 'I had some algebra to finish, then some Spanish . . .'

Remember I told you that Neila is super smart? Well, the reason she's sometimes late for practice is she's SO smart she takes extra lessons after school.

I KNOW!
EXTRA LESSONS.
HOW RUBBISH IS THAT?

As if there aren't already enough lessons at school! I can't even imagine trying to learn MORE. My brain can only just about hold in all the stuff we get taught in the daytime. If my mum and dad made me do EXTRA lessons, I think my brain would overflow and all my intelligence would spill out on to the floor!

Apparently, the teachers think Neila's already smarter

MUSIC

than most grown-ups. The thing is, as incredible as Neila's brain is, I know that most of the time it's full of thoughts about only one thing . . .

I was a little worried about how tonight would go after the incident with the Boneheadz at wet break – but I think we made a major band breakthrough. When the mouse came out to watch us play, Neila managed to dial her ~~stage~~ audience fright down from level ten to about a seven. And Bash managed to play for a whole twenty minutes without looking at his space books and magazines *once*.

And me? Well, I don't know if it was Mr Lloyd's lesson about music in space, or maybe even Bash banging on about stars and aliens at the start of practice – but I wrote a song about space.

It's called . . . **'THE GREATEST BAND IN THE UNIVERSE'!**

The song popped into my head when I popped to the toilet. I didn't have my book of rock with me, so I grabbed one of Mum's eyeliners from the bathroom cabinet and scribbled the lyrics down on these few sheets of loo roll.

THE GREATEST BAND IN THE UNIVERSE

by George Racket

A long, long, very long time ago,
Or so the legend is told,
There was an awesome band who
  loved to rock
And they were only ten years old!

They played real loud; they played real fast.
The best, no ifs or buts.
'Who was this band?' I hear you cry.
The answer, my friend, is US!

- -

We're the greatest band in the universe,
The best in the galaxy.
We're rock stars who rock the stars.
Nothing stands in our Milky Way.

We're the greatest band in the universe
And all our lyrics rhyme.
Even gravity can't pull us down . . .
We're light years ahead of our time!
Light years ahead of our time!
Light years ahead of our time!

I burst back into the garage and rushed over to Bash and Neila, who at first thought it was a little odd that I came running back from the loo waving a piece of toilet paper around over my head..

I picked up my trusty Cosmo and started singing my idea to them, and they both fell silent.

Bash grinned excitedly. 'That is the best song you have **EVER** written. But, to be honest, I thought that as soon as I heard the word *universe* in the title.'

'It is your best song,' Neila agreed. 'Even better than the one you wrote earlier. We should play this at the Battle of the Bands!'

'Battle of the Bands?' Mum said, poking her nosy head into the garage.

'Yeah, we're entering tomorrow,' Bash said.

'The first prize is front-row tickets to see Max Riff and the Comets on Saturday night,' I added.

Well, the moment those words hit my mum's ears it was like someone flicked a switch. Did I mention that my mum and dad are **HUGE** Max Riff and the Comets fans too? Well, they are – and they even met at one of their concerts. If it wasn't for Max Riff and the Comets, I wouldn't have been born! Another reason they're the most awesome band ever.

'**MAX RIFF TICKETS!**' she squealed, and Dad came running in.

'Who's got Max Riff tickets?' he said.

'No one! Not yet, anyway. Whoever wins the school Battle of the Bands wins tickets to see Max Riff,' I explained.

'Oooh, this is exciting! What are you going to wear for the battle?' Mum asked.

The three of us looked at each other and shrugged.

'Clothes . . . ?' I said.

'You can't just wear normal clothes onstage!' Dad said, laughing.

'You're rock stars. You need an image! You need **STAGE OUTFITS!**' Mum said dramatically.

'*Stage outfits?*' Neila said, sounding as confused as I was.

'Yes! Outfits that you wouldn't wear anywhere else apart from onstage!' Mum explained.

Dad laughed again. 'You wouldn't see Max Riff buying loo roll in the supermarket, with his hair as wild as a lion, wearing his massive sunglasses, and leather jacket flung over his shoulder showing off all his tattoos, would you?'

'I wish!' Mum added.

'That's because that's his *stage outfit*. Rock stars are probably walking among us doing normal, everyday things all the time. We just don't recognize them because they're not dressed like rock stars!' Dad said.

'So, what are we going to wear?' Neila asked. I thought she was starting to look a little bit excited, and I suddenly wondered whether a stage outfit might help her to feel more confident when we performed. If it would help Neila, I was totally up for trying it.

'Tattoos?' I suggested.

'**YES!** I've always wanted one!' cheered Bash.

'Absolutely not!' said Dad.

'It should be something that lets people know who your band is straight away, just by looking at you, before you've played a note!' Mum said. 'So, who are you?'

Neila and I looked at each other.

'I've got it!' cried Bash.

He grabbed his copy of *We Are Not Alone*. Flicking through it, he stabbed a finger at a picture. It was an astronaut in a jumpsuit, wearing a helmet, gloves and boots. On the front of the jumpsuit was a name badge: **PEAKE.**

'Why do you want us to dress like that?' Neila said, clearly not impressed with his (lack of) style.

'We're called The Earthlings, aren't we? So we should dress as astronauts, from Earth,' Bash explained.

'I love it!' cheered Mum.

'Very clever,' Dad said.

Bash and Neila looked at me.

'You know what? This could work,' I said slowly. 'We'd have to lose the helmet, or I wouldn't be able to sing . . .'

'And I can't play in gloves,' Neila added.

'Right,' I said. 'But the jumpsuit? That's actually pretty cool.'

Bash was beaming now. 'With our names on the front? Ooh, we could even have our Earthlings logo on the back!'

'Say no more. I'll get my sewing kit!' Mum was already running back into the house. She'd always loved making me fancy-dress costumes when I was a little kid – I even won the Halloween fancy-dress competition four years running!

Dad dug out some dusty overalls and Mum set to work creating our first-ever stage outfits, while we spent the rest of the evening learning how to play 'The Greatest Band in the Universe', until it was time for Neila to head home. And I'm not saying we actually sounded like the greatest band in the universe, but the mouse in the wall seemed to enjoy it. I even heard Mum and Dad humming along.

Are we ready to rock the socks off Greyville School's Battle of the Bands and win those Max Riff tickets?

I don't know, but we're going to find out . . .

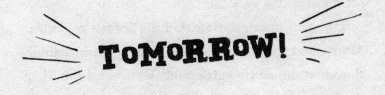

TOMORROW!

TRACK 7

TOMORROW

Mum kicked the morning off triumphantly by making me and Bash 'good luck' pancakes for breakfast. She only ever does that when my friends sleep over, so I bet Bash thinks she makes me pancakes every day.

I WISH!

'Why does Bash get more than me?' I complained, seeing his extra pancake.

'He's our guest, darling. Guests always get extra!' Mum said, smiling brightly, while Bash happily shovelled the entire extra pancake into his mouth as noisily as he could, letting the sticky syrup run down his chin.

'You're so gross,' I said.

'Boys, no fighting today. It's your big concert!' Mum said.

'Actually, Mrs Racket, fighting is what all the best

bands in the world do. This is exactly what we should be doing today. You should probably give me one more pancake just to *really* wind George up,' Bash replied, smiling hopefully.

Mum obviously thought he was joking, because she just laughed and there was no sign of another pancake. 'You two have always been so different,' she said, leaning over and ruffling our hair. 'Ever since you were tiny. That's what makes you such a good match, you know. The sunshine and the rain don't cancel each other out. Together, they make rainbows!'

Bash looked at me as if to say, 'Dude, your mum's embarrassing!' and I replied with a look that said, **'I KNOW!'**

'Well, break a leg today. Can't wait to see you play your first-ever show!' Dad said before taking a long sip of tea.

'What? You're coming to watch?' I said, spitting out my pancake.

'Of course! Wouldn't miss it! Your mum even made us T-shirts to wear.' And, with that, Dad pulled up his jumper to reveal **THE WORLD'S MOST EMBARRASSING T-SHIRT** with the absolute worst photo **EVER** of me, Bash and Neila that Mum forced us to have taken last Christmas at the school nativity.

'You *cannot* wear that,' Bash blurted, but after noticing the shocked look on my mum's face he quickly added, 'because . . . my parents will be **SO** jealous!'

'Oh, don't worry about that! I made some for your parents too!' Mum beamed, pulling out two more of **THE WORLD'S MOST EMBARRASSING T-SHIRTS!**

'Will we finally meet Neila's mum and dad? I could quickly make them T-shirts if you think they'll be there. Didn't you tell me they were musicians too?' Mum asked.

'I dunno . . .' I slurped as I licked my plate clean of maple syrup. I've never actually met Neila's parents. She always goes a little quiet when I ask about them, but she let slip once that they are both musicians. That explains a lot. It must be where Neila got all her talent.

I'm not sure what I got from my parents, but I really hope it's not Dad's hairy ears. Then again, at least I'd never have to buy earmuffs.

'I've put your stage outfits in your bags, and one for Neila,' Mum said, and with our tummies full of sweet, stodgy awesomeness and heads full of songs, I threw my guitar case on to my back, Bash pulled on his backpack, and we jumped on our bikes and headed to school for the big day!

Neila was already at her desk reading the chunkiest textbook I'd ever seen when I arrived in our form room.

'Fancied a bit of light reading before class?' I said, laughing.

'Something like that . . .' she mumbled.

I stood staring over her shoulder, trying to see what she was reading.

'Could you breathe any louder?' she snapped.

I took a deep breath and held it.

And held it.

And held it some more.

Until I was as red as a tomato.

'OK, breathe!' Neila smiled as I sighed in relief. 'Sorry, George. Guess I'm just feeling a bit nervous about later.'

I crouched down, peered over the top of my glasses and looked her straight in the eyes.

'After we win the Battle of the Bands, you'll never have to feel nervous again. You won't even have time, Neila. You'll be too busy rocking the world! It all changes today!'

It changes at 2.30 p.m. today, to be precise, in the main hall. The hallways are already buzzing with excitement. The whole school is talking about it. Kids are running around like a stampede of wild stallions, ready to have their socks rocked off. If stallions wore socks, obviously, which they don't, because they have hooves. It's pretty cool knowing that the whole school will be there to watch us play our first gig!

The school bell is ringing. Time for our first lesson.

The countdown

to ROCK

has begun!

TRACK 8

THE BATTLE OF THE BANDS

Something happened at the Battle of the Bands.

Something big.

Something impossible.

Something . . . out of this world!

I need to write all this down before I forget how it happened . . .

As soon as the 2.30 p.m. bell rang, Neila and I left the English classroom – where we'd had our last lesson together – and met up with Bash in the corridor outside the main hall, where the battle was taking place.

The place was **HEAVING** with people. Teachers, students, parents. It felt as if Greyville School was at the centre of the universe, and everyone was ready to watch the battle.

Inside, a couple of bands were already soundchecking. That's when a band checks that all their equipment and instruments are working properly. Usually the lead singer shouts, **'ONE-TWO! ONE-TWO!'** into the microphone, but we never count higher than *two* in soundcheck. It's an unspoken lead-singer rule. Maybe it's for good luck. Or maybe we're just really bad at counting.

BOOM. BOOM. BOOM.

A deep thumping of drums made the walls rattle with rock, and my excited heart started beating in time. I was raring to get onstage.

'So this is it!' I grinned excitedly as we headed into the cafeteria, which had been turned into a makeshift backstage area. 'Time to suit up!'

I unzipped my bag and pulled out our freshly customized stage outfits.

'Whoa! Your mum must have been up all night!' said Neila as she pulled her astronaut jumpsuit on over her clothes.

'Yeah, once she gets that sewing machine out, there's no stopping her!' I smiled proudly, looking at all the new details Mum had added to the costumes.

Here's what they looked like:

I have to admit, I was bit worried about this at first, but seeing us all suited up and ready to rock in these outfits made me feel a little different. I didn't feel like ordinary George Racket any more. Now I was rock star George Racket!

I started to tune up my bass guitar.

'Have you seen who's on before us?' Bash said, pointing at the running order that was stuck on the wall.

My eyes ran down the list to our name and saw that the band before us was . . .

THE BONEHEADZ!

'Oh no! We have to follow the Boneheadz?' Neila sighed.

'Yes, you do!' came the smug voice of Alfie Biffson from over my shoulder. 'Those Max Riff tickets are as good as ours. You should probably just quit now.'

'No way. You're going to get out-rocked,' Bash shot back.

'Out-rocked? Have you seen how many fans we have out there?' Alfie boasted.

'I don't think you can call them fans if you've

bullied them into cheering for you,' I replied.

Grinning, Alfie pushed the cafeteria door open a crack, and we saw that half the crowd were wearing **BONEHEADZ** T-shirts. My heart sank as I saw that Mr Biffson was handing them out. When he'd pressed the final T-shirt on someone's granny, he leaped on to the stage and grabbed the microphone.

'Parents, students, rock fans – welcome to Greyville School's Battle of the Bands! Each band will have three minutes' stage time. The harder they rock and the louder you scream, the higher they'll score on the **ROCK-O-METER!**'

Mr Biffson pointed to a giant measuring device on the wall next to the stage, with a needle that wobbled from left to right. Beside that was a board with the names of all the competing bands, ready to be arranged in order.

'The band with the highest rock-o-meter reading

wins, but in the event of a tie the winner will be decided by . . . you guessed it: **ME!**' Mr Biffson took a bow.

'There's no way you're getting a higher score than us on the rock-o-meter,' Alfie chuckled while slicking his hair back with a *squelch*.

A sudden cheer came from the crowd in the hall, and Mr Biffson announced the first act through the microphone.

'Please welcome to the stage . . . **DJ D-TENTION!**' he boomed, and the audience whooped as Davey Thomas from Year Four ran onstage.

The battle had begun.

Time backstage seemed to fly as though someone had pressed fast-forward on the world. Band names were shooting up and down the leader board as the rock-o-meter readings were coming in. Bands were disappearing through the stage door one after another to cheers and whoops from the crowd beyond, and I knew that it wouldn't be long until . . .

'It gives me great pleasure to present the reigning

Battle of the Bands champions, returning to defend their title. Please give it up for the most rocking kids in the whole school . . . the **BONEHEADZ!**' Mr Biffson roared, and the crowd went wild as his son strutted out on to the stage followed by the rest of the band.

'ONE! TWO! THREE! FOUR!'

Alfie screamed, and the Boneheadz launched into their song – 'Feel It in Your Bonez'.

All the other bands ran to the side of the stage to watch them defend their title. The walls seemed to shake and the windows rattled as the Boneheadz blasted out some sick chords and riffs while leaping around the stage.

'They . . . actually . . . rock!' Neila whispered, not

able to take her eyes off them.

I hated to admit it, but she was right. There was a reason I'd once thought they were the (second) best band ever! The Boneheadz had the whole crowd jumping up and down. Even my mum and dad seemed to have forgotten which band they were meant to be supporting.

My heart wasn't thumping excitedly any more. It was doing that nervous fluttery thing it does on Sports Day when I'm about to run a race that I know I'm going to lose.

The crowd suddenly erupted with applause, snapping me back to the hall, where the Boneheadz had just finished playing and Alfie Biffson had leaped into the audience and was crowd-surfing over their heads.

The dial on the rock-o-meter shot straight past the previous bands' scores and kept  rising . . . and rising . . . and rising! The crowd were getting louder the higher the dial went, and it didn't stop until it hit the maximum rock level: **OUT OF THIS WORLD!**

'That's the highest score so far! The Boneheadz are in the lead!' Mr Biffson announced.

Neila, Bash and I looked at one another. The Boneheadz' performance was over, which meant only one thing – **WE WERE NEXT!**

We made our way backstage to pick up our instruments and have one final tune up when . . . **DISASTER** struck.

'Oh no! I broke a string!' Neila gasped and, sure enough, there was a strand of silver flapping around uselessly from the neck of her guitar.

'Do you have a spare?' I asked.

'Yes, but it'll take me a few minutes to change it.'

'We don't have a few minutes – listen!' Bash said as the crowd in the hall started chanting, **'WE WANT MORE! WE WANT MORE! WE WANT MORE!'**

Suddenly the Boneheadz burst into the backstage area, high-fiving each other. Then Alfie spotted the broken string.

'I wouldn't even bother trying to change that if I were you. It won't make you sound any better,' Alfie jeered.

Mr Biffson suddenly appeared at the doorway to the hall, clipboard in his hand.

'Great job, Boneheadz. I think you've got it in the bag!' he said, grinning at Alfie. 'Now, Earthlings? It's showtime!'

'What do I do? I can't play with a broken string!' Neila panicked.

'Not to worry,' said Mr Biffson. 'I've got just the thing.'

Seconds later, we were walking out into the hall. I led us to the stage and stepped out into the spotlights. They felt as bright and hot on my face as the sun on holiday, which I guess is why rock stars always wear sunglasses!

Thankfully, the lights were so bright I could barely see Mum and Dad's embarrassing T-shirts. At least, I couldn't until Mum pressed a button and revealed that she'd sewn the fairy lights from the garage into them too, and they now lit up like two Christmas trees.

But embarrassing parents were the least of my worries. We had a show to play and there were Max Riff tickets to be won. This was the time to focus. Our moment. Our one chance to prove that we could be an actual, real rock band!

Bash climbed behind the drums, still wearing his trusty backpack loaded with spare drumsticks (just in case he bashed the pair he was holding a little too hard). He adjusted the stool, pulled the hi-hat a little closer, then played a little roll on the snare, getting a feel for the kit.

I pulled Cosmo's strap over my head, plugged it into the amp and all the little awesome sparkly bits in the cosmic-green paint did their awesome sparkly thing, sending out little beams of rock-light into the crowd like a disco ball . . . only way cooler. I heard the buzz of electricity from the huge bass speaker that towered over me, the biggest I'd ever played through, and even though I wasn't playing any notes yet there was a gentle hum of power vibrating from it.

AWESOME!

I opened my book of rock and laid it on the floor with the lyrics to 'The Greatest Band in the Universe' facing me.

Neila, however, was looking far less ready to rock. She plugged in the school guitar and retreated behind her fringe.

'Psst . . . Neila . . .' I hissed across the stage. I saw one eye glance at me through her hair. 'You ready?'

She shrugged.

That would have to be good enough.

'Bash, ready?' I whispered.

There was no reply.

I turned round and found him gazing out of the hall window as if he was in a trance.

'*Bash?*'

'I . . . I . . . I saw something in the sky,' he said without blinking, without even taking his eyes away from the window.

'OK. Great. Can we talk about that **AFTER WE HAVE PLAYED?**' I said, nodding towards the packed hall in front of us. The crowd was getting fidgety.

'No, seriously,' Bash said, still staring at the sky through the window. 'Look!'

Neila and I followed his gaze and saw that there was actually something in the sky. It looked like burning clouds in the shape of two letters: an **M** and a **V**.

'I think it's a UFO!' whispered Bash excitedly.

'This is not the time for one of your science-fiction stories! Let's play!' I said, putting the weird burning sky letters out of my mind as I turned to face the waiting crowd.

'Hi!' I boomed into the mic. My voice echoed around the room along with a deafening screech of feedback, and the crowd all clapped their hands over their ears.

'Sorry. Sorry!' I said, backing away from the mic a little. I decided to start again. 'Hi! We are The Earthlings, and this is "The Greatest Band in the Universe".'

I held for applause. There was none. Not even from my mum and dad.

There was only one thing to do: **PLAY!**

TRACK 9

BEAM ME UP

My indestructible fingers pressed the thick E-string of my bass guitar and I jumped into the air, kicking one leg out to the side, just like Max Riff did in the music video for the Comets' song 'Leap!'.

I felt as if I was moving in slow motion as I soared over the stage like a rock legend. I remember thinking to myself, *Wow, George, you must have really nailed this sick rock jump, dude. I bet it looks awesome!* – because **I KEPT GOING UP!**

Now, I'm no scientist, but even wannabe rock stars know how gravity works.

What goes **UP** must come **DOWN!** Right?
WRONG!

I kept going. Up and up. Higher and **HIGHER!**

Then I thought, *This is cool, George, but you'd better start going down soon or you won't land on the stage in time to sing the first line of the song.*

But gravity was definitely taking a day off, because I still kept going **UP!**

I looked over to stage left (stage left is always on your left when you face the audience) and saw that Neila had leaped into an awesome rock jump too. She was doing the classic 'splits in the air' jump and her hair was fanned out like she'd been electrocuted.

AWESOME! Surely this was scoring us some serious points on the rock-o-meter?

But then I noticed that Bash, who should have been sitting on his drum stool, was floating in the air too – which is an odd place to be for a drummer. It was as if someone had filled his backpack with helium and it was lifting him up over his drum kit, his sticks clenched tight in his fists. He was looking as confused as I was starting to feel.

Something weird was happening, but as Max Riff always says:

THE ROCK NEVER STOPS.

Which I think is his way of saying *the show must go on*. So I just carried on as though this was all part of our show. Suddenly I saw my mic-stand approaching my face and thought, *Phew! I'm finally landing on the stage!*

WRONG AGAIN.

I wasn't going *down* – my microphone was rising *up* to meet me in the air above the stage, along with my book of rock, which floated past my face as if we were bobbing around in zero gravity! I stretched my arm out and grabbed it before my songs floated out of reach, and I noticed the spotlights starting to get hotter and brighter, until I could hardly see the crowd at all, just the silhouettes of arms in the air and hands throwing the rock sign and, at the back of the room, the faint red and green lights from my parents' embarrassing T-shirts.

That's when I noticed something else.

The audience weren't moving. And the lights on Mum and Dad's shirts weren't flashing.

They were all totally **FROZEN**, as if someone had hit pause on reality.

'What's happening?' Neila called out.

'I don't know! This is weird!' I replied.

But things were about to go up a notch on the weird scale, as suddenly a ring of bright blue energy sliced through the ceiling and surrounded the three of us like a lasso of lightning.

Right above our heads was a circular hole, as if someone had cut a sunroof into the school hall – except we weren't looking at a sunny sky. Instead, it was something vast and dark and as sparkly as my cosmic-green bass guitar.

'What on earth is that?' I yelled.

'I don't think that's on Earth!' Bash shouted.

There was no time to dwell on his mysterious dorky observation. The ring of blue energy surrounding us started to buzz and vibrate as if someone was revving a car, and suddenly . . .

zooM!

We shot straight up through the black hole in the ceiling in what I can only describe as a tube of blue light. It was like being sucked up through a giant blue straw!

'AaaaaaaAAARGH!' Neila screamed – or maybe it was me screaming! – as we looked down and saw the frozen school disappearing beneath our feet.

Then I could see the whole town! All the little rooftops of the houses, the supermarket, Fred's – home of the best battered sausage and chips ever – and its rival right next door (Ed's).

Then in a matter of seconds we could see the whole country. London, Birmingham . . . er . . . Manchester? I knew I should have paid more attention in geography!

Suddenly I realized I could see far more than towns and cities. I could see whole countries and oceans and then the curvature of the **WHOLE PLANET!**

'What's happening?' I shouted at Neila and Bash

as the three of us (and our guitars and drums!) were slurped up the tube of energy, getting faster and faster as the giant buzzing blue straw began twisting and spiralling its way through our solar system.

'*Was that Mars?*' Neila screamed as we swished past a red planet.

'Yeah, and that's Jupiter!' yelled Bash, pointing his drumstick at the enormous ball of brownish gas that we were rapidly approaching. 'Did you know you could fit over a thousand Earths inside Jupiter?'

'This is not the time for a science lesson! **WE'RE IN SPACE!**' I shouted, but my voice was drowned out by the powerful hum of whatever force was sucking us along this blue wormhole across the solar system. We zoomed past Jupiter in a split second, then did a lap around the rings of Saturn, went under Uranus, over Neptune and . . .

'What's that?' I called to Bash, spotting what looked like a cloud up ahead.

'I thought this wasn't the time for a science lesson!' he shouted back smugly.

'Bash, what is it?!' Neila snapped.

'All right, all right! It's the Kuiper Belt!'

'A belt? What for? In case the sun's trousers fall down?'

'It's a giant asteroid belt at the edge of our solar system!' Bash yelled.

Just when I thought we couldn't get any faster, the tube around us started fizzing and sparking and making a noise as if it was charging up, then – **ZAP!**

We were gone in a flash, slicing through the Kuiper Belt at the speed of light, our tube of energy or electricity or whatever it was that was shielding us obliterating any asteroids in our path.

FIZZ! BAM! BLAST!

We left our solar system behind and rocketed out into deep space.

Then deeper space.

Then deepest, darkest space.

Everything went black. Like when Dad first turns off my bedroom light at night-time and at first I can't even see my hand in front of my face.

Then out of the darkness came a teeny dot of yellowish light.

'There's something up ahead!' Neila cried, pointing to the spot at the end of the wormhole.

'We're getting closer!' I said as the glowing dot got **BRIGHTER** and **BIGGER**, and we soared across the universe to somewhere that no band from Earth had ever been before.

TRACK 10

THE SPACE STADIUM

THWACK!

We came to an instant stop, my face slamming into the floor, but it wasn't the warm, well-trodden wood of the school stage. No, this was cool, shiny and black, and as smooth as glass.

My bass guitar had landed next to me and this book – my book of rock – was lying just over a metre away. I scrambled to my feet, grabbed them and held them close as the electric blue force that had sucked us here began to fade, as though it was powering down.

Bash sat up, as one of his cymbals spun round like a spinning penny before crashing to a stop.

'That . . . was . . . **AWESOME!**' he cheered.

'Where's Neila?' I asked.

'Here!' she groaned, poking her head up from the other side of Bash's drum kit, her hair all frizzy as if she'd been electrocuted.

'What just happened?' I asked.

'Three words: **CLASSIC. ALIEN. ABDUCTION**,' Bash said, dusting himself off.

'This is no time for messing around!' I snapped. Even though I'd just seen the planets of our solar system whizz by with my own eyes, there was no way it could have been real.

Bash fell silent and I instantly felt bad. 'Sorry, Bash,' I said. 'OK. Let's think. All right, so we got beamed up. Now what? How are we going to get back to the battle and play our set and . . .'

The last of the blue force around us finally disappeared, and a strange hissing, swishing sound came flooding in.

'Is that the ocean?' I asked.

'I don't think that's water,' Neila replied, cautiously rising to her feet. We turned and saw that the hissing sound wasn't waves; it was **APPLAUSE**.

From the biggest crowd I had ever seen.

We were in the middle
of what looked like an
ENORMOUS stadium. It was like the World Cup
Final – times a million! It made Max Riff's live
stadium concert look like one of our band practices
in the garage.

I realized we were standing on a circular stage that
seemed to be hovering thirty metres in the air, like a
flying saucer.

Bash looked at me with his 'I told
you so' face.

Then he said it out loud,
just in case I didn't understand
the look.

Suddenly more tubes of bright, sparking
blue light beamed down from above, just
like the ones that we had travelled through, and
several flying-saucer stages fizzled into existence out
of thin air and were hovering around us.

The cheering crowd went wild, and it was only
then that I noticed that the audience was made up of
hundreds of thousands of . . . creatures.

All right, I'll say it.

ALIENS!

Wait. It's so bonkers I've got to write that again.

They were aliens!

Actual extraterrestrial, outer-spacey, flying-saucery, we-really-are-not-alone, I-can't-believe-Bash-was-right-all-along **ALIENS!**

How did I know they were aliens?

Believe me, I just knew. And you would have known too. For starters, there were the ones with tentacles that were flapping about in the air, clapping their suckers together. Then the ones with orange wibbly-wobbly antennae poking out of the tops of their heads, *boing*-ing around. There were some with hundreds of eyes, and others with just one big boggly eyeball. There was slimy skin, scaly skin, translucent skin, glowing skin, and a few with no skin at all!

I'd never seen creatures like them before in all my life. But there was no time to stop and take in this bizarre sight, because those fizzing blue tubes around us were fading, just like ours had, revealing what was inside them.

Yep. You guessed it.

MORE ALIENS!

They all staggered to their feet – well, at least the ones that *had* feet did – and took in the sight of the ginormous space stadium, looking as mesmerized as we had looked about twenty seconds before. Then they all started to see the other saucer-shaped stages floating around them and the lifeforms on board.

'Is that a-a-alien trying to c-c-communicate with me?' I stuttered, gawping at a creature on the neighbouring saucer. It had the legs of a spider – a giant hairy orange spider – large crab-like claws and two long feelers poking out of what I guessed was its head. Weirdest of all, it was most definitely waving one of those feelers at us.

'Affirmative!' Bash replied.

'Well, you're the space nerd! What do I do?' I whispered.

'Just smile and wave back!' Neila said.

So that's what I did. I smiled and waved. At an **ALIEN SPIDER-CRAB CREATURE**.

It jumped excitedly, clacking its spidery legs on the hard floor of its saucer, and making a strange noise with its mouth. At least, I think it was a mouth!

'What's it saying?' I asked Bash.

Bash shrugged. 'How am I supposed to know?'

But somehow all the other aliens were now chatting to each other in what must have been dozens of strange new languages. There were robotic **BEEPS** and **BLARTS**, deep rumbling **GROWLS**, high-pitched melodies, **CLICKS** and **CLACKS**. It was total chaos, but there was something weirdly awesome about the mish-mash of sounds.

'Look, I think our spider-crab friend is pointing at something,' I said, noticing that our neighbour was frantically waving an orange claw at the floor of our disc.

'What are these things?' Neila said, scooping up something flat and rectangular from near her feet.

'Those look like . . . **BACKSTAGE PASSES!**' I exclaimed, taking one and examining the pass.

It was black with holographic foil writing, like those shiny football cards some of the other kids at school collect. There were just two letters on the front, which the three of us recognized instantly – **MV**.

'The letters in the sky!' we whispered together.

I looked around and saw that all the other aliens had already put their passes on.

'I guess we're meant to wear them?' Neila said, slipping hers over her head. Just as she did so, her mouth fell open in disbelief.

'No way!' she gasped. 'You've got to hear this. Put your pass on!'

I quickly put the shiny pass over my head and the moment it fell round my neck all the strange alien voices surrounding us changed. They weren't speaking strange alien languages any more. They were speaking English – and I could understand them perfectly!

'No way!' Bash gawped. 'Translation passes! I've read about this technology in *We Are Not Alone*, issue three hundred and seventy-six! These are **SO** cool!'

'So this means I can understand anything anyone says?' I asked.

'Yeah! As long as you're wearing that pass, it'll automatically translate what anyone says into the language of whoever is wearing it. **PRETTY AWESOME!**'

'Greetings, creatures from another world!' a chirpy voice called out. 'Can you understand me now?'

It was Crabby, the alien with the pincers.

'Er . . . yes! Hi!' I said, and we waved at each other.

'Whoa, you just made contact!' Bash whispered excitedly.

'From which galaxy do you originate?' Crabby asked.

'We're from Earth, in the Milky Way,' Bash said, with the biggest grin on his face.

'Wow! Well, you've travelled far, creatures of Earth. We're from Crustacea, in the Tidalious Galaxy,' Crabby said.

'**COOL!** What's it like there?' Bash asked, hanging on to Crabby's every word.

'Deliciously salty!' put in another crab-like creature that was clacking around the saucer from Crustacea.

I quickly counted, and saw that there were four of them in total. The first one we'd spoken to must have noticed me looking at his friends.

'How rude of me! Allow me to introduce my band,' the crab alien said. 'This is Steve, this is Beverly, and that's Joyce. And I'm Dave.'

'Steve? Dave?' I laughed. 'We get beamed across the universe and the first aliens we meet are called Steve, Beverly, Joyce and Dave?'

'No, no, no, you don't get it!' Bash shook his head at me. 'Those aren't their *real* names. It's just the translation pass turning them into names that our human brains will understand!'

'Oh! I get it! **CLEVER!**' I grinned. 'But hang on – did you just say that you're a *band*?'

'That's right!' replied Dave. 'We're called The Pincers!'

I shook my head at how crazy this was. 'We're a band too!'

'Well, of course you are. Why else would you be here?' said Dave. 'We're *all* bands!'

And, with that, he gestured with his pincer to the flying discs surrounding us, and I looked closer at the groups of creatures moving about on them. It was only then that I noticed that loads of the aliens had what looked like musical instruments! Some of them looked familiar. There were guitar-like instruments with glowing strings, and things being banged like drums, but there were other instruments unlike anything I'd ever seen before, and I wouldn't have even been able to guess what noise they made.

The three of us Earthlings could have stared at all these alien bands for light years, but darkness began to fall across the stadium as though the lights were being purposefully dimmed for the start of a show, and somewhere from the shadows of space a deep voice boomed:

'WELCOME!'

TRACK 11

MEGAVOLT

The crowd of extraterrestrials went extra wild, whooping and waving their tentacles and antennae and suckers and . . . other bits of alien anatomy that I didn't even know the names of!

'WELCOME, ALL! WELCOME!' the voice boomed again as spotlights sliced through the blackness of the super-stadium and swooped over the crowd, who were all chanting something . . .

'MEGAVOLT! MEGAVOLT! MEGAVOLT!'

'What's a Megavolt?' Bash asked Dave, who seemed to have become our first alien friend.

'*What's* a Megavolt?' Dave spluttered as though Bash had said something absolutely ridiculous. 'It's not *what,* but *who*! You mean you don't know about the champion?'

We shook our heads.

'Well, you're about to find out.'

There was a sudden explosion of blue lightning bolts and several hundred thousand alien eyes (and three pairs of human ones!) turned to see that they had struck what looked like an enormous, epic stage, a hundred times bigger than the discs on which we were all standing.

The chanting got louder and more intense . . .

'MEGAVOLT! MEGAVOLT! MEGAVOLT!'

Then – *BOOM!* – a blast of blindingly bright energy beamed into the stadium, and a giant glob-like creature materialized centre stage.

His skin was acidic orange and glowed like hot lava, with drops that hissed and spat as they melted through the stage floor.

'So I'm guessing that's Megavolt . . .' I whispered to Bash, whose mouth was hanging open like a gawping fish. I glanced at Neila and saw that her eyes were wide.

The crowd had reached a whole new level of hysteria.

'People seem to really like him!' I said to Dave.

'Like him? Everyone is terrified of him!' Dave

replied, looking around to check that no one else could hear.

'Terrified? Why?' I asked.

'You'll see . . .' said Dave.

'What?' I blurted, but Dave didn't get a chance to say anything else before Megavolt opened his molten mouth to address the audience.

'HELLO, UNIVERSE!' Megavolt roared in a voice so terrifically loud that it rattled our saucer. Hundreds of huge screens appeared around the stadium and Megavolt flashed up on all of them, so that there was no escaping his blistering hot face.

'Welcome to the loudest, the wildest and the *deadliest* competition in the universe!' he boomed. 'It's time for the ear-splitting, planet-pulverizing

INTERGALACTIC
BATTLE OF THE BANDS!'

'Did he just say **BATTLE OF THE BANDS?**' I hissed.

'Er, George, I think you might be focusing on the wrong detail here,' Bash said, gulping. 'Did he just say **PLANET-PULVERIZING?**'

'We are aboard the Space Stadium, beaming live to billions of galaxies from the orbit of my home, **SPECTRA!**' bellowed Megavolt.

The crowd went crazy as Megavolt threw his glowing arms wide, commanding the roof of the stadium to slide open, revealing that we were on the edge of what looked like a vast, dark . . . nothing.

'What's that?' I said in utter disbelief.

Bash gawped. 'That's a supermassive black hole.'

'That's Spectra. Well, that's what's left of her!' croaked Dave.

The three of us whirled round to face him. 'Her? You mean, that black hole was a . . . person?' I asked.

'You mean, you've never heard of Megavolt and Spectra?' Dave said.

'No!' we replied together.

And then Dave told us a story that sounded as if it could have come straight out of one of Bash's space comics . . .

ROCKSTAR WARS: VOL. 1

In a distant world and a distant time, there were two stars — rock stars. They were called **MEGAVOLT** and **SPECTRA**, and for a long time they were the biggest stars in the cosmos.

Everyone in the galaxy loved them, but they especially loved Spectra. She was light years ahead of her time . . .

and had always shone a little brighter than Megavolt.

Her stardom grew . . . and grew . . . and grew . . . until she was such an enormous star that she couldn't handle the pressure any more. Spectra collapsed and vanished, leaving behind a supermassive black hole where she'd once shone.

Megavolt is never very far from being pulled into the enormous vast nothingness where Spectra used to be. So Megavolt began the Intergalactic Battle of the Bands to reignite his stardom. And there's not a single band in the universe that can stop him . . . or is there?

I had a billion questions I wanted to ask Dave, but another very enthusiastic one-eyed alien bounced on to the stage wearing a dazzling suit jacket that sparkled like pink stardust.

'Thank you, Megavolt, Your Mightiness! And hello, universe! I'm Quark Blisterbum, and I'll be your host for this legendary battle,' Quark Blisterbum said through the permanent cheesy smile that was plastered on to his green face. 'Now, for anyone who has been living inside a black hole, let's recap the rules!

'Sixteen brave bands have been carefully selected from sixteen different planets from the deepest reaches of the cosmos.'

A brilliant beam of light suddenly shone down on us. Once my eyes adjusted, I saw that there were spotlights on all the saucers hovering around the stadium – sixteen in total.

'These bands will battle against each other (musically, of course!) to try to prevent their planet from being **ECLIPSED!**'

The crowd exhaled an excited 'Oooooooooh!' as

holograms of each band's home planet appeared over their saucer. I glanced up and saw a projected Planet Earth spinning above our heads.

'*Eclipsed* . . . What does that mean?' I whispered to Neila, but she just shrugged.

'When a band is knocked out of the competition, their planet is *eclipsed*. This happens one by one until there is just one band remaining.' As Quark explained, dark shadows suddenly fell over all sixteen hologram planets.

'The last band rocking will return to their planet at the **EXACT** moment they left – as if nothing ever happened!' Quark announced, still smiling.

'*The exact moment we left – as if nothing ever happened.* That's impossible!' I said, trying my best to get my brain around these rules.

'Well, not impossible, actually,' Bash said. 'If they can harness the quantum flux and manipulate the universal time coordinates of the –'

'**THIS IS NOT THE TIME TO TRY TO EXPLAIN TIME TRAVEL, BASH!**' I said as Quark continued.

'However, all the *eclipsed* planets will be . . .' Quark paused dramatically.

The eclipsed hologram planets were suddenly zapped by some sort of gravity beam, and zoomed across the stadium like meteors. They appeared to crash right into Megavolt's massive molten mouth, and he pretended to munch on them all like cosmic snacks.

The crowd erupted into crazed cheering and squeals of excitement, but as I squinted at their alien faces I couldn't help but feel that they all looked a little scared.

'*What?*' I blurted. 'You mean, we're in a battle of the bands and, if we don't win, Earth will be . . .'

Dave gulped. 'Megavolt munchies!'

'UNLESS,' Quark said, calming the crowd, 'the winning band decides to use . . . the **GRAVITY GAMBLE!**'

The stadium gave another excited 'Oooooooh!'

'The winning band can choose to return safely

home OR risk it all with the Gravity Gamble and battle the mighty Megavolt himself in the Grand Final!' Quark said, bowing before the behemothic Megavolt. 'If they win, not only will they be crowned the Greatest Band in the Universe – but **ALL SIXTEEN PLANETS** will be saved and everyone will return to their home!'

We hadn't played a single note yet and the aliens in the crowd were already chanting, '*Gravity Gamble! Gravity Gamble! Gravity Gamble!*'

'OK, so we just have to rock harder than all the other bands, use the Gravity Gamble, defeat Megavolt, then everyone's planet will be saved and we all get to go home?' I said. 'Er, does anyone else not have a good feeling about this?'

'And that's not even the worst part!' Dave clicked.

'How can that not be the worst part?' asked Bash.

'No one has ever beaten Megavolt in the Gravity Gamble! He **ALWAYS** wins!'

Dave, Steve, Beverly and Joyce trembled.

Neila looked as if she was going to be sick.

I felt as if I was going to be sick.

Bash *was* sick.

I couldn't believe this was happening. A few hours ago, I was in the kitchen eating pancakes with maple syrup, chatting to my mum. Now I was in outer space, on the edge of a supermassive black hole, about to music-battle a bunch of aliens to fight for the survival of our entire planet.

What a weird Wednesday!

While the rules of this Intergalactic Battle of the Bands were still fresh in my brain, I thought I'd scribble them down in my book so I didn't forget them.

SIXTEEN BANDS battle
to save **SIXTEEN PLANETS**

When a band is knocked out,
their planet is **ECLIPSED!**

The band that's still **ROCKING** at the end
gets to go home, and all the eclipsed planets
are **EATEN** by Megavolt!

UNLESS . . .

The winning band decides to **GRAVITY GAMBLE** and music-battle Megavolt himself.

If they **WIN**, all sixteen planets are saved and everyone gets to go home.

If they **LOSE**, ALL SIXTEEN PLANETS become **MEGAVOLT FOOD!**

A huge futuristic throne-like seat rose out of the stage and Megavolt slopped into it like a molten space slug. Once he was comfortable, Quark Blisterbum made an announcement that reverberated around the stadium:

'LET'S MEET THE BANDS!'

TRACK 12

THE BANDS

One by one, each flying-saucer-shaped stage began to whizz into the centre of the stadium so that the audience could get a good look at the bands . . . including US!

'Quick, you should write everyone's names down in your new diary!' Neila said.

'Neila! It is NOT a diary! This is my book of rock!'

'Whatever. If we're battling these aliens, we need to remember as much as we can about them, work out their weaknesses!' she explained.

I don't know when Neila became such an expert on how to defeat aliens, but she did have a point, so I pulled out my pen and began to quickly sketch them in my book of rock, which is definitely **NOT** a diary.

'From Planet Corrodia, let's hear it for

8-TRAX!'

said Quark Blisterbum, and a rusty robot gave a jittery salute to the crowd, leaving a trail of metallic red dust hanging in the air.

'Up next, all the way from Snotopia, the sloppiest singing duo in the bogeyverse, it's

SLIMEBLOB AND GLOOP!

'Fighting for the survival of Nauticalia, the ocean moon they call home, it's Squiddle, Squaddle and Squish:

THE SQUID SISTERS!

. . . followed by a band who need no introduction. Hold your noses and unplug those scent receptors, because things are about to get stinky! From the depths of Uranus, it's

THE GASSY GIANTS!'

'*The Gassy Giants?*' Bash squeaked. 'George, I told you that was a good band name!'

'That's so gross!' Neila said, gagging.

'Better out than in, I always say!' I replied.

'Hold the pyrotechnics, because the next band are highly flammable . . .' announced Quark. 'It's the fuzziest rock band this side of the Milky Way. Give it up for

THE FURRY WURZLETS FROM SNORFLE!'

And the spotlights hit a band of four creatures covered from head to tail in candyfloss-pink fur.

'Didn't we eat one of them at the funfair?' Bash joked.

'I must have hit my head because I'm seeing double! No, wait — it's the two-headed sensation beaming in all the way from the moon called Croon.

Let's hear it for

MICHAEL DOUBLÉ!'

continued Quark.

'Now, hide your sugary snacks, folks! Racing in from Planet Hypa, a world made entirely of sugar cubes, it's the band of brothers who never sit still . . .

go berserk for **BUXY!**

'Then it's the eight-bit band from Digitropolis. Give it up for **PIXEL SHIFT!**'

As Quark Blisterbum announced their name, the band of three pixelated aliens rearranged their shapes and morphed into three identical copies of Quark himself!

Bash gasped. '*Shape-shifters!*'

'Awesome!' I whispered.

Neila gulped. 'Yeah, unless we have to battle them!'

I'd completely forgotten that we might have to go up against any of these bands. Before I could start to panic again, Quark was already introducing the next group.

'From the harmonic hills of the dreamiest edge of the galaxy, grab an oxygen tank because Planet Manufac-Tur's boy band will take your breath away!

IT'S OZONE!

'Next, give it up for

THE BIG BANGS!'

'I think I should probably be in that band,' said Bash.

'Surfing the sun all the way from the six-string star system called Shred, it's the rock star from the stars! Go wild for

STAR GIRL!'

At Quark Blisterbum's announcement, the coolest-looking rock-star alien I could imagine slung her star-shaped guitar over her shoulder and did an epic knee slide across her flying-saucer stage, which spun underneath her like some sort of intergalactic Frisbee.

'She's got moves like Max Riff!' I said.

'Yeah, but cooler,' Bash teased.

'No way!' I replied . . . although she was pretty awesome. She even wore glasses, like me, only hers were star-shaped ones! AND they were **COSMIC GREEN! (I KNOW!)**

'Now for some mystery!' Quark Blisterbum said dramatically, and the stadium lights dimmed. 'From the far side of an uncharted planet in an unknown galaxy, let's hear it for legendary opera star

DARK MATTER!'

A large cloaked figure floated silently in the centre of their saucer, not moving a single muscle! Only their eyes could be seen glowing from the shadows under their hood.

'I hope we don't have to battle them!' Neila whispered.

'Me too!' I replied.

'Me three!' agreed Bash.

'Moving swiftly on,' said Quark, 'from a shadowy opera star to a jazz band that have been touring the universe for so long that they can't even remember where they're from. I give you:

ELLA TERRESTRIAL AND THE SAXOPHONE HOME ORCHESTRA!'

Quark cheered, and the spotlights swished to another saucer stage, where the most glamorous singer stood. She wore a gown that sparkled as if it was bedazzled with actual stars, and her backing band blasted into oddly shaped trumpets and saxophones.

'Next! They're small, they're grey, they'll beam you up in the night – all the way from Zeta Reticuli,

IT'S **U.F.O.!**'

Quark cried, and the whole crowd started chanting, '**U.F.O. – U.F.O. – U.F.O.!**'

'Those aliens are called Greys!' Bash said. 'We've got one of their UFOs at Area Fifty-one!'

Area 51 is a mysterious top-secret military base in the USA that Bash (and *We Are Not Alone*) is convinced is packed with aliens and alien spacecraft that have crash-landed on Earth. Whenever Bash starts waffling on about the UFOs there, I usually tell him it's a load of nonsense. This time, though, as the group of bulbous-headed grey aliens zoomed past on their hovering stage, I decided to keep my mouth shut.

'Watch your toes – those claws are sharp! From Crustacea, it's **THE PINCERS!**'

There was only one band left to be announced. Us! 'And finally, from Planet Earth, please welcome

THE EARTHLINGS!'

Quark Blisterbum boomed, and the crowd went wild as our flying-saucer stage swooshed into the spotlights in the centre of the Space Stadium.

BOOM!

Megavolt slammed his glowing hot fist on to the arm of his metallic throne and silence fell across the stadium.

All eyes were on him as he opened his molten mouth and roared:

'LET THE BATTLE BEGIN!'

TRACK 13

ROUND ONE: ROCK-OUT TO KNOCK-OUT

Our saucer lurched forward, and I scrambled to grab my book of rock and bass guitar before they slid over the edge. We began orbiting the stadium with all the other flying discs, circling round and round over the heads of the screaming crowd below.

Suddenly two of the saucers began descending to the stadium floor. They became two stages facing each other, ready for battle.

'On Stage One, *iiiiit's* **8-TRAX!**' announced Quark Blisterbum as the lights focused on the rusty robot. The crowd whooped and cheered and started chanting the robot's name '**8-TRAX! 8-TRAX! 8-TRAX!**' And as he gave them a wave, a screw came loose in his rusted wrist and his hand fell off! The crowd cheered even louder as he scrambled to screw it back in, and the commentator announced his rival.

'On Stage Two, give it up for the **SQUID SISTERS!**'

The spotlights swooshed over to the tentacled aliens, one of whom was now sitting at a drum kit holding not one, not two, but *eight* drumsticks. Another had her tentacles wrapped around a microphone, and the third had an electric guitar, a bass guitar and keyboard grasped in her suckers. All three of them had their eyes focused on **8-TRAX** as if he was some sort of prey that they were about to devour.

'This is Round One: **ROCK-OUT TO KNOCK-OUT!**' Quark Blisterbum declared. 'Winners go through to the next round. Losers lose . . . *every*thing! 8-TRAX, you're up!'

8-TRAX flicked a switch on his chest and his rusty robotic limbs clanked and clicked.

'I can't watch! He's going to fall apart!' Neila said, hiding her eyes.

But it turned out that 8-TRAX had some tricks up his sleeves . . . literally! His whole body transformed into what looked like DJ decks, and he suddenly blasted out a beat that had the entire stadium on their feet! Then a door flung open in his rust-ridden chest to reveal a mini robot, who leaped out with a mini microphone in his mini hands, and started rapping.

It was one of the coolest things I'd ever seen, and it went something like this:

YO, YO, MIC CHECK . . .

THIS IS MY PARTNER – HE'S CALLED 8-TRAX –
AND I GO BY THE NAME OF MINI-JACK!
I MIGHT BE SMALL, HE MIGHT BE RUSTED,
BUT IF YOU BATTLE US, YOU WILL GET BUSTED.

I'VE GOT THE RHYMES; HE BRINGS BEAT.
THERE'S NOT A SINGLE ALIEN WE CAN'T DEFEAT.
NEVER UNDERESTIMATE THIS PAIR OF DROIDS.
WE'LL HIT YOU HARD LIKE ASTEROIDS!
WE'RE OUT OF THIS WORLD, EXTRATERRESTRIAL,

BUT KEEP IT TO YOURSELF COS IT'S CONFIDENTIAL.
MY LYRICS ARE SO fly THEY CALL THEM CELESTIAL.
SO HARD TO BELIEVE THAT IT'S EXISTENTIAL.

SO DON'T BE FOOLED BY MY RUSTY EXTERIOR,
COS WHEN IT COMES TO RHYMES I'M SUPERIOR.
BEAM US UP AND WE WILL BATTLE TILL THE END.
WE'VE GOT A PLANET THAT WE WILL DEFEND!

Then Mini-Jack started rocking some head spins on the floor, unscrewing his metallic joints and reconfiguring his robotic limbs, throwing shapes and moves that I'd never seen before – all while 8-TRAX scratched some beats on the decks.

As they performed, a huge device was illuminated on the stage and a dial started rising, higher and higher the louder the crowd cheered.

'It's like the rock-o-meter at school!' Neila realized, pointing to the giant cheer-measuring device.

'**THEY'RE AWESOME!**' I cried.

'They've got to win this!'

But suddenly the spotlights swung over to the Squid Sisters, and silence fell in anticipation.

'**ONE! TWO! THREE! FOUR!**' the drummer – Squiddle – screamed, before crashing into the most unbelievable drum solo I've **EVER** heard. There were drumsticks flying all over the place and even though she had eight tentacles it looked like eight hundred. She tore around the kit so fast it was just a blur.

Then her bandmate – Squish – began to sing, and the final Squid Sister – Squaddle – joined in, playing the bass guitar . . .

AND lead guitar . . .

AND the keyboard . . .

ALL AT THE SAME TIME!
(I KNOW!)

As her tentacles slid along the fretboards of the guitars, her suckers found chords on the keys that I'd never known existed. The noise was so intense it started blasting bits of 8-TRAX's rusted body away.

'Oh no!' I gasped.

The galactic rock-o-meter raced up the scale.

'The Squid Sisters win!' announced Quark Blisterbum, and the stadium burst into deafening applause.

8-TRAX and Mini-Jack huddled close as holo-screens around the stadium all suddenly displayed a rust-coloured planet. A big red button rose out from the stage in front of Megavolt.

'I don't think I want to know what that button's for,' Bash whimpered.

'I can't watch!' muttered Neila, covering her eyes.

I couldn't tear my eyes away from 8-TRAX and Mini-Jack. Even the Squid Sisters had gone quiet now. I felt super bad for them too. It wasn't their fault; they'd done what they needed to do.

Megavolt raised his lava-like fist into the air and held it teasingly over the big red button, and the crowd began to chant, **'ECLIPSE! ECLIPSE!'**

He obeyed and slammed his blistering hot fist down, hitting the button. The stadium shook like an earthquake as an enormous

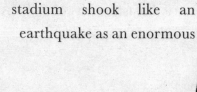

laser cannon fired what looked like some sort of beam of shadows out into space. A few seconds later, everyone watched the screens as the same shadow-beam hit Corrodia, home to 8-TRAX and Mini-Jack.

'What is that thing?' I whispered to Bash, who was gawping at the black laser beam.

'That's black-hole energy!' he muttered in disbelief. 'I've read about it in –'

'*We Are Not Alone.* Of course!' I said, finishing his sentence, as suddenly a thick cloud of this black-hole energy engulfed the planet, extinguishing all light, until all that could be seen of Corrodia was a sphere of darkness floating among the stars.

Now, maybe it was just my mind playing tricks on me, but as the light of Corrodia was eclipsed by this strange shadow-beam, Megavolt's molten body seemed to glow a little brighter, like the burning embers of the fire Dad made that time we went camping, which seemed to come back to life in the breeze.

'Well, folks, we have our first eclipse!' Quark beamed, seeming to relish the sight of the dark planet. '8-TRAX and Mini-Jack are out of the battle. Their only hope of saving Corrodia now is for the winner to choose the Gravity Gamble.'

'Ooooooh!' sang the audience.

'But it's not Megavolt's feeding time just yet! There are still more battles to be rocked before Megavolt gets his feast!' Quark teased as Megavolt clapped his glowing hands together and boomed:

TRACK 14

NEXT!

The rounds that followed were unbelievable.

We heard the pitch-perfect harmonies of Ozone echo around the stadium while they backflipped and breakdanced, but they were up against the Big Bangs, who smashed out ground-breaking beats that made Ozone's head-spinning routine fall to pieces.

The Gassy Giants parped their gross green gas into weird-looking trumpets that sounded like . . . well, like a brass band of bums. The stink was so intense that Ella Terrestrial and her Saxophone Home Orchestra were too totally grossed out to even play!

Michael Doublé had the whole stadium crooning along with him – until Star Girl rocked one of the best guitar solos I've **EVER** heard.

Pixel Shift defeated the mysterious, hooded Dark Matter by shape-shifting into identical copies of the opera singer. As Dark Matter belted out unthinkably powerful operatic notes, Pixel Shift instantly analysed and replicated them, so that if Dark Matter sang higher, they sang higher too. If Dark Matter held a note longer, so did they! Finally Dark Matter was outnumbered and out-opera'd . . . by themself!

The Furry Wurzlets defeated Buxy, because the band of brothers had stuffed their face with so many sweets from the Space Stadium snack stand that they had an intense sugar rush and played their song so fast that it was over in only three seconds.

U.F.O. performed a song called 'Take Me to Your Leader', but they were out-rocked by The Pincers' feel-good melodies. Our crabby friends seemed to magically hypnotize everyone into feeling as if they were on a relaxing beach holiday – until disaster struck . . .

CRACK!

The Pincers' drummer, Steve, got carried away and his crab-like pincers sliced right through his drumsticks!

'Oh no! They're done for!' I gasped.

'No, they're not!' Bash said, unzipping his trusty backpack full of nerdy space comics and . . . yep, that's right! *Spare drumsticks!*

'Hey, Steve! **CATCH!**' Bash yelled as he launched the sticks across the stadium and right into Steve's claws, just in time for him to nail an epic drum fill that knocked U.F.O. flying out of the competition.

All the defeated bands watched their planets get eclipsed, just like Planet Corrodia, waiting to become mega-snacks for Megavolt, who was definitely glowing brighter and hotter with each world he plunged into darkness.

My heart began to race as I realized that soon it was going to be our turn. That's right. Us. Just three kids from Earth. We were going to go head-to-head

against a band of aliens to try to
stop the world from being eclipsed
and becoming Megavolt's lunch!

How were we going to get
through? I saw Neila staring around before looking at
the battered school guitar in her hands, and I knew
she was thinking the same thing.

'It's impossible!' Neila sighed.

'No, it's not! We can do this! We **HAVE** to do
this! Planet Earth is counting on us. We're their only
hope!' I said.

'No pressure, then,' Bash added as Megavolt
blasted another shadow-beam through space and
eclipsed another helpless planet.

'NEXT!' he growled, and the crowd cheered.

Our saucer suddenly dropped towards the stadium
floor.

'It's us!' I shouted over the roar from the crowd as
Quark Blisterbum's voice echoed around the stadium.

'From Planet Earth, please welcome **THE
EARTHLINGS!** And they'll be battling . . .
SLIMEBLOB AND GLOOP!'

We watched as another flying disc swooped down to meet us in the centre of the stadium. There sat the two blobs of bogey-like jelly, looking like the sort of pudding we're served up at school lunchtime.

They had no arms.

No legs.

No faces.

Just two wobbly blobs.

Suddenly the spotlights fell on us, along with the watching eyes of hundreds of thousands of aliens.

'Well, this is it!' I said, throwing Cosmo's lightning-bolt strap over my head. *What would Max Riff do?* I wondered, hoping for a bit of last-minute inspiration. But I realized that Max Riff had never been abducted by aliens or had to play for the survival of his planet. Even he couldn't help me now!

We were on our own.

'What song shall we play?' Bash asked, taking his place behind his drum kit.

'Let's play "The Greatest Band in the Universe"!' Neila said. 'It's our best song! And it's the song we were just about to play when we were beamed up!'

I nodded and turned the volume dial on my bass up to ten. This was it. Our moment.

'**ONE! TWO! THREE! FOUR!**' Bash yelled, and I blasted into the intro of the song. All the tiny little hairs on the back of my neck stood up as I didn't just *hear* the sound of my bass; I *felt* it, the power of it, echoing around the massive stadium.

Out of the corner of my eye, I saw the rock-o-meter shoot up the scale. Bash smashed an epic fill around the toms and it zoomed up even more.

WE WERE ROCKING!

I looked over to Neila as she placed her hands on the splintered fretboard, her fingers ready to blast out an almighty E major chord that I knew would make the crowd go wild. She raised her plectrum in the air – but as she brought it down to meet the strings, something moved on the saucer opposite us.

Slimeblob and Gloop were suddenly wobbling and expanding. They began to swell and grow into huge gelatinous beasts that towered over us!

The spotlights swooped over to shine on our rivals, leaving us in the shadows.

'Hey, we're still playing! Isn't this against the rules?' I called over the roaring crowd.

'I don't think there are any rules!' Neila said as giant gooey arms began to grow from Slimeblob's and Gloop's blobby bodies. What looked like faces seemed to emerge, and where the two school puddings had once sat were now two enormous snot aliens.

And they looked ready to defeat us!

Slimeblob grabbed a handful of jelly from . . . his own bum **(I KNOW!)** and stretched it out like Play-Doh to make something.

'It's a guitar!' Neila gasped – and she was right. He was now holding a jelly guitar!

'Just keep playing!' I shouted, but it was no use. The crowd had stopped listening to us, and were chanting, '*Slimeblob! Slimeblob! Slimeblob!*'

He strummed the stretchy strings of snot gel on the

guitar he'd made from his bottom, and the most disgusting sound drowned out our song, forcing us to stop and cover our ears.

'No!' I shouted. 'We – have – to – keep – playing!'

I grabbed hold of my bass and started plucking away, trying to pick up the song where we had left off – but now the other jelly creature, Gloop, pulled out a chunk of his own wobbly body and began making something else. A microphone on a long, stretchy jelly cable. He started swinging the mic around in the air, performing all sorts of awesome tricks.

The crowd went crazy.

'The rock-o-meter!' cried Neila as the dial instantly rose.

Then Gloop started singing.

Well, it was more like that sound your tummy makes when you're really, *really*, **REALLY** hungry. It's the noise where gurgle meets bum-trump.

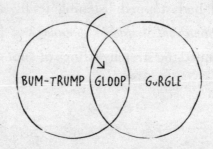

Despite this sound being almost unbearable to hear, the fact that these snot-resembling creatures had dared to interrupt our performance had scored them some serious points on the rock-o-meter, and we were being left behind. We needed a miracle or Earth was doomed!

That's when I noticed the first bubble appear. It started somewhere deep inside Slimeblob's gloopy body and bubbled up to his head, where it went **POP!**

Then another bubble appeared . . . **POP!**

Then another, and another, until his whole head was bubbling like the kettle when Dad makes a cup of tea.

'It's the spotlights!' Neila shouted. 'They're too hot!'

Boiling bubbles started appearing in Gloop's body too, and both their jelly bodies started to melt like candle wax!

Their song slowed down and the crowd began booing, and the dial on the rock-o-meter plummeted. In a matter of seconds, the intense heat from the spotlights had **TOTALLY** melted the jelly aliens into two steaming puddles of slime on the stage, and their song slopped to an end.

'THE EARTHLINGS WIN!'

Quark Blisterbum yelled, and the crowd went crazy.

While alien roadies swept up the puddles of Slimeblob and Gloop into buckets, Megavolt shadow-beamed their planet, Snotopia – which looked like a ball of blue jelly – and a few moments later the sloppy sphere was drenched in deep shadows to the delight of the roaring crowd.

And that's how we only just made it through Round One.

TRACK 15

PEET-SA

After the sixteen bands had battled in Round One, there were only eight left – including us – and Megavolt had eclipsed eight whole planets that were now on the menu for the final feast!

'Earthlings! Earthlings!' called Dave, waving a crabby claw at us as our saucer rose slowly from the stage to take its place beside The Pincers. All four spider-crab aliens were lined up, and seemed to be waiting for us.

'You saved us from certain elimination, Earthling drummer Bash. We are forever in your debt!' Dave said.

'Oh! No big deal. I always carry loads of spare drumsticks!' Bash shrugged and smiled.

'No big deal?' they repeated, before they burst out into a crazy noise that I realized must be laughter. It sounded like this: **'KLARK! KLARK! KLARK!'**

'What's so funny?' asked Bash.

'You said saving us was *no big deal*, but on our planet that would be a very BIG deal. We now owe you a **LIFE DEBT**.' Dave smiled. At least, I think he smiled. It was hard to tell; after all, he was a spider-crab alien.

'What's a *life debt*?' Neila asked.

'Oooh, I've read about these! It's like a promise, just one you can't ever break!' Bash explained.

'It's much more than a promise.' Dave chuckled. 'A life debt is the most ancient and powerful promise of our people. It means that we are now sworn to protect you and your kind from any harm.'

'Honestly, you really don't have to do that,' Bash said.

'Oh, but we have no choice. Just take a look at your arms and see for yourself,' Dave said.

The three of us rolled up the sleeves of our flight suits and discovered that we each had a black mark on our skin in the shape of a pincer.

'What is *that*?' Neila shrieked, trying to rub the mark off.

'There's no use trying to rub it off. It is the mark of the life debt you are owed. It will only disappear once the debt has been repaid,' said Dave.

'So this is basically . . . **A TATTOO?**' I said, feeling a massive grin spread across my face.

'Space travel **AND** tattoos! This is the **BEST DAY EVER!**' Bash cheered, admiring his new alien ink. 'All right, then, life debt it is. I'll let you know when we need it!' And he leaned over and shook claws with Dave.

Now that the first round was over, our saucers whizzed backstage and we were escorted from them by a tiny little droid called Beep-Bop. At least, I'm guessing that was its name, because it kept saying, 'Follow Beep-Bop. Follow Beep-Bop,' then making a *beep-bop* sound and whizzing along in front of us.

We left our instruments for the alien roadies to take care of, but I kept my book of rock closely tucked under my arm, knowing that I'd want to write all this down before I forgot it.

Backstage was like the place I'd always dreamed it would be. Well, in my dreams we were backstage on Planet Earth . . . but, still, there were huge cables running along every bit of floor, flight cases covered in stickers that looked like they'd toured the universe hundreds of times, alien roadies bustling about with alien guitars and microphones and trumpets under their arms, and the whole place was buzzing with excited energy.

'Where are we going?' Neila asked.

'Follow **BEEP-BOP**,' Beep-Bop beeped again as it whizzed deeper into the Space Stadium and towards a set of metallic doors, which swished open, releasing the strangest smell my nostrils have ever sniffed. It was as if someone had cooked every type of food I could imagine all at the same time!

'What is this place?' Bash asked, sniffing the air – but I already knew exactly where we were. I recognized it from the *Max Riff Backstage Tour* documentary, and remember him saying:

Welcome to every rock star's favourite place on tour . . .

I grinned excitedly. '*This* is Catering!'

'Eat. **BEEP-BOP.** Eat,' Beep-Bop blooped and we stepped into the cavernous hall, packed with tables that were already crowded with crew and our alien competitors, stuffing their faces with the most unusual-looking food.

Bash beamed. 'I'm starving!'

'Space travel makes you hungry!' Neila added.

'Ha, sounds like you do this all the time,' I joked, and she grinned.

'Yeah, I mean, I guess it must have been the space travel.'

A short, round blue alien suddenly appeared behind the rows and rows of food laid out in trays.

'Come in, come in! Grab a plate. Help yourself!' the alien said, pointing at the selection of food with one of his four arms and a proud smile. 'I'm **GARBLE**, the head chef here at the Space Stadium. We want to make you feel as comfortable as possible, so we've created a selection of traditional dishes from the home planets of all the bands in the battle. Allow me to show you. Here we have freshly squashed snart from the moon of **SNORFLE** . . .

'Or perhaps you'd prefer roasted gloople tart?

'Or, if that's not to your liking, then why not taste barbecued tail of trodent? It's been aged for twenty-four light years.' Garble beamed with pride.

'Snart from Snorfle? Gloople tart? Tail of trodent?' Bash said, screwing up his face like he'd smelled a trump. 'That all sounds absolutely di–'

'Delicious!' Neila interrupted quickly, before Bash could say something that might offend Chef Garble.

I joined in with Neila. 'Oh yes, it all sounds absolutely delicious! But, er, do you maybe have anything from Earth?' I asked politely.

'Earth! Yes, yes, yes! Of course!' With that, Garble darted along the display buffet of trays, reading labels and throwing them in the air.

'Uranus . . . Corrodia . . . nope. Zeta Reticuli . . . Crustacea . . . Aha! **EARTH!**' Garble cheered. 'Yes, I remember now! I must say, I have been a chef for a thousand years and this is the most peculiar dish I have ever cooked!'

'Oh no, what's it going to be?' Neila whispered nervously.

'I don't know, but I hope it's not one of our five a day!' Bash replied.

'From Planet Earth we have something called . . . **PEET-SA**,' Garble said enthusiastically.

Bash, Neila and I looked at each other and shrugged.

'Peet-sa? I've never heard of it!' Bash said.

'Me neither!' Neila and I replied – but when Garble lifted the lid on the tray labelled **EARTH** it all made sense.

'Peet-sa!' Garble repeated, wafting away the delicious-smelling steam clouds that filled the air to reveal the biggest, most incredible-looking . . .

'PIZZA!' we exclaimed.

'Yes! Like I said, **PEET-SA!**' Garble grinned.

We grabbed a slice each and took a mouthful of the cheesiest, warmest, gooiest, stuffed-crustiest pizza we'd ever tasted.

As we chewed, we couldn't help grinning cheesily at each other.

Planet Earth was still in one piece.

We'd completed Round One of the Intergalactic Battle of the Bands, and, just for a moment, we felt like champions.

And we were gobbling the most delicious pizza in the entire universe.

Things were looking up for The Earthlings!

'Excuse me, but may **WE** try a piece of your peet-sa?' asked a polite voice.

It was Dave, clicking his pincers excitedly. In fact, all the other remaining space bands were gathered around, desperate to try this strange Earth food.

'Sure! There's plenty to go round!' I said.

'Really?'

'Yeah! That's the best thing about pizza. It's made to share!' I said, and we handed slices to everyone.

'It's amazing!' clacked Dave.

'It's incredible!' sang the Squid Sisters, who had a slice in each tentacle.

Slimeblob and Gloop had reset into shape after melting under the intense spotlights, and now slid their way over to our table.

'Sorry about the whole melting thing,' I said, handing them a slice each. 'And . . . you know, your planet being eclipsed.'

I really did feel bad about that, but Gloop was shaking his head. 'No hard feelings, Earthling.'

'That's the way this competition goes,' Slimeblob squelched, and he took the slice of pizza and slopped it on his head, where it started to sink into his jelly-like skin. We all watched it make its way down to his stomach and dissolve, creating a **BIG BUBBLE** that rose back up to his head – and out came a huge

Everyone cheered and laughed.

Then one of the crab-like aliens – I think it was Beverly – did a huge

too!

Then the Squid Sisters burped together at exactly the same time, and suddenly all the aliens started belching and burping.

Bash, Neila and I looked at each other and smiled before joining in the **INTERGALACTIC BURP-FEST** too.

It was awesome! Gross, but awesome!

'Bet this isn't in *We Are Not Alone*!' I said to Bash.

'Nope!' He burped again and patted his belly.

'If you want any more peet-sa, just say the word and I can deliver a slice right to your dressing room!' Garble said.

'ROOM SERVICE IN SPACE?' Bash said.

'Oh yes! I deliver food to everyone on this ship. The artists, the crew, the crowd. That's why I'm the only one Megavolt trusts with a key that opens every door!' He held up a glowing key card. 'For food-delivering purposes only, of course!'

'Hang on. Did you just say that we have our own dressing room?' I asked.

'Of course! All bands through to the next round have dressing rooms!' Garble laughed.

Once the last crust of peet-sa had been gobbled up, and we'd belched our last burp, Beep-Bop returned.

'Follow Beep-Bop. Follow Beep-Bop,' it beeped, and everyone obeyed, following the little droid with bellies full of deliciousness. We passed glowing signs on the backstage walls until we reached a long corridor lined with eight star-shaped doors, and Beep-Bop bleeped, 'Welcome to your dressing rooms.'

TRACK 16

SPACE SLEEPOVER

Beep-Bop led us down the corridor.

'*Beep-bop*. The Squid Sisters,' Beep-Bop bleeped, and the first star-shaped door swooshed open to reveal what looked like an aquarium with a huge tank filled with purple water.

(PURPLE WATER! I KNOW!)

When Bash came on holiday with us once, Dad told us that if we peed in the swimming pool it would turn the water purple to alert the lifeguard and they'd have to shut the pool to clean it!

I'll be honest – I've peed in almost every pool I've ever swam in and none of them have turned purple, so I'm pretty sure Dad was lying – but I'm still not going to be swimming with the Squid Sisters any time soon.

'*Beep-bop*. You must remain in your dressing rooms overnight. Anyone that leaves will be automatically disqualified and their planet pulverized,' beeped Beep-Bop.

The tentacled triplets slithered inside, plunged into their potentially pee-filled purple pool, and the door swished shut.

'*Beep-bop*. The Furry Wurzlets,' Beep-Bop called, and the next star-shaped door slid open. An explosion of pink fur flopped out into the corridor. Inside, it looked like a forest of pink fluff with fluorescent flowers flowing in a simulated breeze. The equally pink and furry band disappeared and – **SWOOSH!** – the star door shut them inside their dressing room and we were moved on by Beep-Bop.

One by one, Bash, Neila and I caught little glimpses of the alien worlds that our rival bands called home.

Dave and The Pincers crabbed sideways into a room filled with green sand.

Star Girl did a knee slide into a room that looked like a rock star's dream, with guitars covering the walls and two windows shaped like her starry glasses, which looked out on to the actual stars.

The Gassy Giants bumbled and trumped their way into a room filled with green bum gas.

Pixel Shift, the shape-shifters, walked into a room that looked like a level in an awesome rainbow-coloured video game.

As their door swooshed shut, I suddenly realized something.

'Hey, where are all the bands who lost Round One?' I asked Bash who, judging by the look on his face, also hadn't noticed their absence. Now that I came to think of it, except for Slimeblob and Gloop, the eclipsed bands hadn't been in Catering either.

But there was no time to dwell on it as Beep-Bop had come to the final doorway.

We were next.

'*Beep-bop.* The Earthlings. Enjoy your stay. *Beep-bop!*' Beep-Bop said as the star door slid open to reveal . . .

'It's our garage!' Bash gasped, dropping his backpack on the floor in disbelief.

'Yeah, only bigger,' Neila added. '**WAY** bigger!'

'And way better!' I said, stepping inside the most ultimate garage any Earth band could dream of!

Firstly, it wasn't cold like our garage at home, and there was no dust or dirt anywhere. The floor was as clean as a dinner plate!

'There's an actual stage!' Neila squeaked excitedly as she spotted a huge practice stage with our instruments set up and ready to rock.

'Mum would love these lights!' I said, admiring the ceiling, which was covered in millions of multicoloured fairy lights – just like our garage back home.

There were cupboards fully stocked with all our

favourite Earth snacks — cheese-and-Marmite sandwiches and peanut-butter chocolate cups for me, crisps for Bash, and even a bowl of steamed broccoli for Neila (which was just a waste of a bowl, if you ask me!).

There was a super-sized sofa in front of a super-duper high-definition TV that was showing cartoons from home, and one whole wall was covered with video-game arcade machines!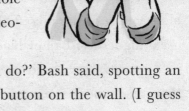

'What does this button do?' Bash said, spotting an impossibly tempting red button on the wall. (I guess Megavolt must really like red buttons.)

'Hang on. It's not going to eclipse Earth, is it?' I said.

'Only one way to find out.' Neila shrugged, reached out her finger and gave the button a push.

Suddenly the huge garage door jolted with the usual metallic **CLANG!** and began to open, allowing a brilliant slice of starlight through the expanding horizontal crack. At first, I worried we were going to be sucked out into space – I'd seen that happen in one of Bash's favourite sci-fi films! – but when my eyes adjusted I realized we were looking through an enormous panoramic window at the most awesome view across the infinite cosmos.

'WHOA!' We all gawped together.

There were billions of stars as far as our human eyes could see, swirling nebulas and galaxies that I'd only ever seen in Bash's dorky space books – and right at the centre of this incredible view was the whopping-great mahoosive ball of blackness.

'Spectra,' Neila said in awe, and I remembered that this was the name of the black hole where Megavolt's superstar bandmate used to be.

'I don't get why everyone makes such a big deal about black holes. Looks like a ball of nothing to me,' I said, shrugging.

Bash looked at me as though I was bonkers.

'That "ball of nothing" is one of the most mysterious and powerful things in the universe,' Bash said.

I had a feeling I was about to get one of his space

lessons. This time, though, I guessed it might be quite useful to listen.

'When a star gets too big and goes supernova –'

'What-a-nova?'

'Supernova! When it explodes! Well, it doesn't just disappear. It leaves something behind . . . **GRAVITY!** An invisible force pulling everything towards it.'

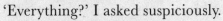

'Everything?' I asked suspiciously.

'EVERYTHING!' Bash confirmed.

'Even . . . light?'

'Of course! Why do you think it's black? Even light can't escape,' Bash said with a smug grin.

I thought hard for a few minutes. There had to be *something* that a black hole couldn't pull in.

'All right, smarty-pants, what about . . . time? It can't suck in time!' I said, feeling pretty confident that I'd caught him out with that one.

'Even *time*!' Bash whispered dramatically. 'The closer you get to a black hole, the slower time moves!'

I won't lie – the whole thing made my head hurt.

As I stared out at the billions of stars and planets ahead of us, I wondered where Earth was. I found myself thinking about battered sausage and chips from Fred's, the *real* garage, Mum and Dad.

Would I ever see any of them again?

'It's out there somewhere,' I sighed.

'What is?' Neila asked.

'HOME!' I said.

I realized Bash had gone quiet too, staring out in the same way that I was.

'Do you really think we can do it? Can we save the world?' he asked.

The truth is I wasn't sure, but I spoke without hesitation – like any good lead singer should.

'Absolutely! All we have to do is beat those bands, save the world and we'll be beamed back to the school hall like we never left.'

'Er, guys . . . when you see what I've just found, you might not even want to go back to Earth!' Bash said, pointing.

He had spotted the coolest part of our dressing room. The only thing cooler than a room with a view into an actual black hole . . .

'*Triple-height bunk beds!*' I stared up at the three stacked space beds, reaching from the floor to the dangling fairy lights above. 'I didn't think these things existed in real life,' I whispered in amazement.

'We're the first humans in history to make contact with life from other planets, on board a spaceship full of actual aliens – and you're finding bunk beds hard to believe?' Neila laughed.

'TRIPLE-HEIGHT BUNK BEDS!' said Bash in awe.

He ran straight over to the bunk beds and I knew he was about to climb straight to the top to try to claim the highest one – because we all know that the top bunk is **THE BEST!**

Well, he *tried* to climb to the top – but quickly discovered that there wasn't a ladder.

'Let me show you how it's done,' I said, running over to join Bash.

The only problem was that I couldn't climb up either. I just leaped up and down like a wally. The top bunk was simply too high!

'That's impossible! No one can reach that!' I scratched my head, looking up to the unreachable top bunk.

'Oh yeah?' said Neila, rolling up her sleeves. She took a big run-up and leaped over our heads.

SPLAT!

Nope. She didn't make it either.

Our dream of triple-height bunk beds was shattered. No wonder you never see them on Earth. They don't work!

Until Bash noticed something: a lever on the side of the bunk beds that said **PULL HERE**.

We jumped for it at the same time and pulled it all the way down together until it *clicked*.

SWISH!

There was a sudden hiss of air . . . and my feet started to leave the floor.

'I'm flying!' I gasped as I floated away from the floor of our spaceship dressing room and towards the ceiling!

'The lever turns the gravity off!

'WHEEEEEEEE!'

Bash squeaked with excitement as he pushed hard off the ground and went spinning through the air.

'Now *I* call top bunk!' said Neila with a grin as she soared towards it.

'No chance!' I yelled.

'It's mine!' shouted Bash.

The three of us laughed and cheered as we pushed and bobbed around the air of the dressing room, walking on the ceiling and bouncing off the walls. Suddenly the top bunk didn't matter. We were all just enjoying being gravity-free: no invisible force pulling us down, no up or sideways – only open space in which to move around.

I did a forward flip over to the cupboard and found a jumbo-size bag of marshmallows – the ultimate sleepover snack (even in space!) – and ripped the bag open, sending pink and white balls of deliciousness floating in the air. We spent the rest of the night flying around catching them in our mouths. At some point, I guess we fell asleep, because the next thing I knew it was morning and I was waking up to the feeling of warm sunlight shining on my face.

'Morning!' Bash yawned from the top bunk.

'Morning,' I replied from the middle bunk.

Neila groaned like a zombie from down below. 'Breakfast. Must. Eat. Breakfast . . .'

Neila was one of those people who had to eat something before she could function like a normal human being.

'Let's see if Garble has left anything for us in the fridge,' I said, hoping there might be some leftover peet-sa.

We all climbed out of our bunks and headed to the big silver refrigerator. When we got close to it, we realized it was covered in a layer of frost thick enough to write in it, like on car windows in the winter.

'It's stuck!' Bash said, yanking on the cool metal handle.

'Let me try,' Neila said, giving it a go, but also failing to open it.

I grabbed hold too and we all pulled together.

CLANK!

The heavy metal door swung open, and a swoosh of cold air rushed out, along with a white cloud of frozen fog.

We wafted it away . . . and discovered far more than breakfast.

Two big round eyeballs blinked open and stared right at us through the icy mist.

There was *something* in the fridge.

Something alive!

TRACK 17

WE ARE NOT ALONE

We ran for our lives and leaped behind the sofa!

'D-d-did you see it?' I spluttered nervously.

'No! I was too busy screaming!' Neila replied.

'What about you, Bash? . . . Bash?'

There was no reply.

Bash wasn't behind the sofa with us!

'Where is he?' I panicked.

'I don't know! I thought he was right with us!' Neila whispered.

Then we heard *it*.

The last sound you want to hear when your friend is missing in a room with a strange creature from outer space . . .

CRUNCH! CHOMP! GULP!

I'm not really sure what happened next. I've never felt it before, but I guess it was my best-friend superpowers kicking in. Without thinking twice,

I hurdled the sofa, closed my eyes and jumped in the direction of the crunching creature, ready to sacrifice myself to save my bandmate from the jaws of the evil space alien.

'Nobody eats my drummer!' I hollered heroically as I slammed my shoulder into the creature's body and tackled it to the ground.

Except it wasn't the strange fridge monster that I tackled . . .

'What are you doing, you big twerp?' Bash winced, pushing me away.

'Sorry! I thought you were being eaten by an alien,' I said, helping Bash to his feet.

'So, if you weren't being eaten . . . what was that crunching sound?' Neila asked, climbing out from behind the sofa.

CRUNCH! CHOMP! GULP!

We heard it again. This time we didn't hide. Instead, we turned round to see that the fridge door was wide open. The creature responsible for the noises was standing silhouetted in the yellowy glow, munching on . . . not Bash but last night's leftover marshmallows.

'Who are you?' I asked, trembling, and the chomping creature paused, turning slowly to face us.

Silently, it stepped closer. I saw a pair of curious, friendly brown eyes and a head of fuzzy black hair. To my surprise, I recognized the creature immediately. I had even drawn his picture just a few days ago.

I grabbed my book of rock, flicked back to my notes from Mr Lloyd's science class and held my sketch up to show Bash and Neila.

'It's Armstrong the Astro-Ape!' I blurted.

And the name badge on his spacesuit confirmed it!

The chimpanzee bounced up and down and clapped with excitement.

'Greetings, children of Earth!'

The three of us just stared at him.

'Er . . . just checking. Did anyone else hear the chimpanzee in a spacesuit talk?' Bash muttered.

'Yep!' Neila and I replied in disbelief.

'Hi!' I said to the chimp. 'Can you understand what we're saying?'

Armstrong reached inside his spacesuit and pulled out his own translation pass, just like the ones we were wearing round our necks.

'Of course! Genius!' Bash said.

'Armstrong is very happy to be reunited with creatures from Armstrong's planet! Tell Armstrong, how is Earth these days? Still in one piece, I hope? What country are you from? So many questions!'

Armstrong leaped around the dressing room, bouncing off the walls and the ceiling excitedly.

'Well, actually, *we* probably have some questions too!' Neila said.

'Oooh, questions for Armstrong! **HOW FUN!** Let me guess: do chimpanzees really like bananas?' Armstrong laughed.

'How did you know I was going to ask that?' I said.

'No! Not *that* question!' Neila said, rolling her eyes at me. 'More like – what happened to the *Minerva Seven*?'

Armstrong suddenly fell silent and looked very concerned.

'Oh, you know about the *Minerva Seven*,' he said, bowing his head sadly. 'It was not Armstrong's fault. Armstrong did what Armstrong was told. Armstrong pressed all the right buttons in the right order. But instead of releasing the special satellite, a big blue fuzzy beam appeared and

ZAP!

The next thing Armstrong knew, the rocket had vanished and Armstrong was aboard this Space Stadium.'

'A big blue fuzzy beam . . .' Bash repeated, looking at me and Neila. 'That sounds familiar!'

'So Megavolt is the reason the *Minerva Seven* vanished!' I realized. 'But . . . that was **YEARS AND YEARS AGO!** Shouldn't you be really old by now?'

'Oh yes! Armstrong should be very old, very old! Armstrong should be a shrivelled, wrinkly, probably dead chimp! But Armstrong sleeps long snoozes in Armstrong's hypersleep pod! Armstrong stays chimpy-fresh.' He smiled a toothy grin, making us all laugh.

'Oh, it's a **HYPERSLEEP POD!** Not a fridge!' I said, looking at the cold silver box we'd thought might contain some breakfast for us.

'But why would Megavolt beam you up?' Neila asked. 'It makes no sense.'

'Megavolt did not mean to beam Armstrong. Megavolt beamed Armstrong by mistakident,' Armstrong explained.

'Then what was Megavolt really trying to beam up?' I asked.

But, before Armstrong could answer, the star-shaped door to our dressing room swished open.

'Follow Beep-Bop. Follow Beep-Bop,' Beep-Bop chattered, and from somewhere in the distance the roar of a huge crowd could be heard chanting something over and over.

'Round Two!
    Round Two!
        Round Two!'

Neila, Bash and I looked at each other.

It was time to go and save the world again.

TRACK 18

ROUND TWO: ROCK TILL YOU DROP

'Eight bands remain. Eight planets at risk! Who will rock? Whose home will be pulverized? Today our bands will face **ROUND TWO** for their chance – should they choose it – to battle the one and only Megavolt in tomorrow's Grand Final. Welcome back to the greatest show in the universe! It's the **INTERGALACTIC BATTLE OF THE BANDS!**'

As Quark Blisterbum made his announcement, we found ourselves rising out of a stage in the dead centre of the stadium, under the massive roof that was open to the stars, surrounded by the roaring crowd. This stage was a giant circle and had been divided into eight sections, like eight slices of pie (or peet-sa).

'One slice of stage for each of the remaining bands,' I whispered to Bash and Neila as, suddenly, those other bands started rising out of the stage too. A huge screen hovering high above displayed the names of the bands ready to battle in **ROUND TWO**.

①	THE FURRY WURZLETS
②	THE SQUID SISTERS
③	THE GASSY GIANTS
④	THE BIG BANGS
⑤	STAR GIRL
⑥	THE PINCERS
⑦	PIXEL SHIFT
⑧	THE EARTHLINGS

Our names looked more like the player-select screen in a video game than a real-life space battle, and I had to keep telling myself,

This is actually happening, George. You're in space!

But I was even finding it hard to believe my own voice in my own head.

'Where are the other bands?' Bash asked. 'The ones who were knocked out yesterday?'

I looked around and realized they still weren't with us. Perhaps Slimeblob and Gloop had been with us in Catering so that they could re-jellify, but now they were nowhere to be seen. Where were they and the other knocked-out bands? Was Megavolt forcing them to wait in a room that constantly reminded them of the planet they'd failed to save? Was I asking too many questions instead of focusing on the battle?

Probably, but I was about to get some answers. The cheers from the crowd suddenly changed to deafening **BOOS!**

'There they are!' Neila said, and pointed to the eight defeated bands as they were ushered into their own section of the stadium. It almost looked like some kind of **SPACE PRISON** – only instead of being behind bars, the bands were being kept behind red laser beams that fizzed and sparked.

'Aww, just wook at the poor wittle ewiminated bands!' Quark Blisterbum said in a babyish voice, pretending to look sad.

'He'd look *really* sad if *his* planet was in danger of being destroyed!' I whispered as the floating screens all flicked to show the eight eclipsed planets, swirling silently in thick, dark shadow.

But, as sad as it was, there was no time to dwell on other planets being destroyed. The deep sinking in my tummy made me realize that Earth could be next – and we could soon be joining them in the *laser-beam prison for aliens without a home*!

'Before we begin, please be upstanding for rock royalty! The reigning champion, the almighty, all-powerful **MEGAVOLT!**' Quark Blisterbum boomed, and the back of the stage split in half to reveal the blindingly hot orange glow of Megavolt as he swaggered into the stadium and slumped his scorching bottom on to his molten throne.

Silence fell.

The whole stadium waited.

'LET'S ROCK!' Megavolt declared.

Our instruments suddenly began to appear right in front of us, as though they'd been beamed in from backstage!

'All right, folks! Round Two is a game we like to call **ROCK TILL YOU DROP!** It's an all-out, non-stop music marathon, and the last four bands rocking go through,' Quark explained.

'"Rock Till You Drop"? What does that mean?' asked Neila.

'It means we don't have to sound good. We just can't stop!' Bash said.

'Then we might have a chance!' Neila said, grabbing the school guitar.

'Start playing,' I yelled, 'and whatever you do, **DON'T STOP!**'

'What song?' Bash said as his drum kit finished materializing around him.

That's when I realized that I had already written the **PERFECT** song to get us through this round. The song inspired by Mr Lloyd's never-ending science class . . .

'"The Longest Song Ever"!' I said.

'Of course!' Neila said, grinning, as I flicked back through my book of rock to page 31 where I'd scribbled the lyrics, and threw it down on the stage between us. We'd only played this a couple of times – in the garage the night before we were beamed up – but I had a good feeling about it.

Neila cracked her knuckles and slung her guitar strap over her shoulder. I turned up the volume dial on my bass to full and gave Bash a nod.

'ONE! TWO! THREE! FOUR!' he screamed and started wildly smashing the drums, while Neila blasted out the only three power chords a rock band from Earth needs – E, A and B.

It didn't sound great. In fact, it sounded pretty awful. But this round wasn't about who could rock the best. It was about who could rock the longest.

I took a deep breath, faced our alien competitors and started singing.

> It's the longest song,
> It goes on and on . . .
> You can sing this song forever!
> The longest song,
> It goes on and on . . .
> When will this song end? NEVER!

'*NEVER!*' shouted Bash and Neila on backing vocals.

With eight bands playing **AT THE SAME TIME**, the noise in the stadium was at eardrum-popping levels. If we were at home in the garage, Dad would have been straight in to tell us to turn it down, but we were in space now and there was a planet that needed saving. This wasn't the time for grown-up health-and-safety sensibleness. Sorry, Mum and Dad!

On the stage around us, the other bands were rocking out too. I could see Star Girl's super-fast fingers twiddling around furiously on the frets of her glistening guitar, which was changing colour as she played.

Awesome!

The Pincers were happily jamming out some melodic beach tunes, and on the slice of stage-pie next to them The Pincers also looked to be happily jamming out some melodic beach tunes . . . That's when I realized that one band must have been Pixel Shift, who'd shape-shifted to look like The Pincers and were replicating their happy-making vibes!

We played and played and played. After what felt like **HOURS** of non-stop playing, I could tell that not everyone was coping well with repeated rocking out. The Furry Wurzlets, on their own slice of pie, looked exhausted. They might have sounded better than us, but there was no way they could keep this up forever.

But us? We could play badly all day.

As the round dragged on and on, I had a feeling it wouldn't be long before the first band dropped out of this rock-out!

TRACK 19

THE FIRST TO FALL!

There was a sudden shudder, followed by the whirring and clanking of mechanical gears, and without warning the stage under our feet shifted. We all lurched and wobbled.

'I think we're starting to spin!' shouted Bash over the booming beats of his drums, and he was right. The whole stage was slowly spinning round like a carousel at a fairground.

It wasn't enough to distract us, though. We kept facing forward. **WE KEPT PLAYING.**

'They'll have to do a lot worse than that to stop us from rocking!' I shouted back to Bash.

I spoke too soon.

The entire stage lifted into the air, rising high over the stadium floor while spinning faster and faster. From a distance I imagined it looked like a giant spinning plate on a stick.

CRACK!

The stage shook under our feet.

'Earthquake!' Bash shouted as we played.

'Don't be ridiculous! We're not on *Earth*!' Neila said.

'All right, *spacequake*!' he corrected himself.

BOOM! There was another shudder from under our feet and I realized that the *spacequake* actually came from the Big Bangs, who had banged and bashed their slice of the stage-pie so much with their big beaters that there was now a narrow crack in the shiny floor!

'A few more beats and they're goners!' Neila shouted.

And she was right!

The crack split wide open under their feet and the Big Bangs fell into it – and out of the competition, landing in the laser-beam prison with the other eliminated bands.

The crowd went wild!

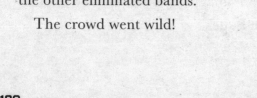

'THE BIG BANGS ARE OUT!'
cheered Quark Blisterbum.

'Now we know why it's called Rock Till You **DROP!**' Neila said as we peered into the gaping hole in the stage opposite us, while still playing.

'GEROFF!' someone growled.

We turned and saw that the Furry Wurzlets had become so dizzy from the spinning stage that they'd got their candyfloss-pink fur tangled together in a knot.

'YOU GEROFF ME!' the other Furry Wurzlet replied, but the more they bickered with each other, the less they concentrated on what they were playing – and it did **NOT** sound good!

TWANG! BOING! GONG!

until they fumbled to a halt.

The crowd started chanting. **'DROP! DROP! DROP! DROP!'**

Megavolt raised his hand and brought it crashing down on to a big, *way-too-dramatic* red button on the arm of his throne, and . . .

W H O O S H !

The Furry Wurzlets' slice of stage suddenly opened and they disappeared from the battle in a blur of pink fur, which gave them a soft, fluffy landing in the prison below.

'The Furry Wurzlets are gone!' cried Quark Blisterbum, and the audience cheered.

There were six bands left now. If two more dropped, we would be through and Earth would be safe for another round! All we had to do was **KEEP PLAYING!**

The same three chords.

The same drum fills.

The same lyrics.

It's the longest song,
It goes on and on . . .
You can sing this song forever!
The longest song,
It goes on and on . . .

Even though we weren't trying to sound good, I realized that the more we played, the *better* we played. As we looped round 'The Longest Song Ever' for what felt like the five-millionth time, we weren't sucking quite as much as we usually did. In fact, we actually sounded pretty average! Which was **GREAT** for us!

Neila threw in some little riffs between the chords and Bash added some new fills he'd not tried before. They were experimenting! Grinning, I took a deep breath and did the same. I once heard Max Riff say:

> YOU'VE GOTTA WALK
> THAT BASSLINE LIKE A DOG
> IN THE PARK.

And as my fingers walked up and down Cosmo's smooth frets, I finally knew what he meant!

Suddenly the stage started spinning faster. And not just a little faster – we were whizzing round like a tornado.

'Just . . . keep . . . playing!' Bash shouted as he smashed the cymbals.

Squish, the lead singer of the Squid Sisters, was slipping backwards towards the edge of the spinning stage.

'All eyes are on the Squid Sisters! Can they hold on, or will they be taking the plunge?' jeered Quark Blisterbum.

Squish slapped all her tentacles on to the stage, trying to hold on – but it was no use. She was just too slippery. She came unstuck and slid all the way to the edge of the stage, wiping out Squiddle and Squaddle on her way, and they all went toppling over together.

'Another one bites the dust as the Squid Sisters join the eliminated! Only one more to go. Who will it be?' teased Quark.

The tension built in the stadium.

This was it.

We were nearly through Round Two!

We just had to hang on and keep rocking until one of the other bands dropped! How hard could it be?

SNAP!

The sound came from somewhere behind me . . .

Somewhere close.

A little too close.

'I BROKE A STICK!' screamed Bash.

I spun round to see **HALF** a drumstick in his hand. He'd rocked so hard that it had **SNAPPED IN TWO!**

'Don't stop playing!' I yelled, and Bash kept the beat going with his foot, stomping on the kick-drum: **THUD! THUD! THUD!**

Now, a lot of people would think: *That's it! They're done for! How can they play without a drummer?*

But not me! I'd seen the *Max Riff Backstage Tour* documentary hundreds of times, and their drummer breaks his drumsticks in pretty much every show. All he does is reach down for his spare set of sticks and then keeps rocking like nothing happened. It always looks **SUPER COOL!**

No big deal!

That's why drummers always have extra drumsticks when they play, and why Bash always keeps his backpack full of spares on him at all times. Handy for when The Pincers had needed them yesterday – and handy for right now.

'Just use the spare sticks in your backpack!' I shouted.

Keeping the beat thumping with his foot, Bash reached behind him – and his mouth dropped.

'My backpack!' He gulped. 'It's not here!'

I turned my head away from the microphone long enough to confirm that there was nothing but thin air in the place on Bash's back where his backpack would usually be!

'I must have left it in the dressing room!' he said.

I didn't say it out loud, but what I was thinking then was: *That's it! We're done for! How can we play without a drummer?*

In the distance, I saw tiny solar flares erupt from Megavolt's mouth as he burst into delighted laughter at our fail. The other bands around us were showing zero signs of giving up . . . all except for the Gassy Giants, whose green stinky trumpets were running out of stink with every trump they puffed.

That's our only hope, I thought to myself. *If only we can hold on for just a little longer . . .*

'Oh dear, oh dear!' I heard Quark Blisterbum say. 'It looks like The Earthlings are in trouble! Their drummer has broken a drumstick and doesn't have a spare! Could this be the final performance for the humans?'

Over the **THUD-THUD-THUD** of Bash's kick-drum I heard the crowd chanting, **'DROP! DROP! DROP!'**

'What do we do?' Neila screamed.

'I don't know . . . Play a solo or something!' I shouted back.

'I can't play a solo on this thing!' Neila said, shaking the school guitar in frustration and retreating behind her fringe.

Megavolt suddenly appeared on the giant screen. We watched as he raised his dripping-hot hand in the air and held it over the big red button, ready to drop us.

'**DROP! DROP! DROP!**' the stadium roared.

'This is it!' Bash said, and a tear ran down his cheek. 'I'm sorry, Planet Earth!'

Megavolt clenched his fiery fist.

There was nothing we could do.

The Earthlings had failed Planet Earth.

Still playing, I closed my eyes, ready for the drop . . .

. . . but it never came.

Instead, the crowd stopped chanting and let out a wild squeal of excitement.

'What's this?' exclaimed Quark. 'A strange creature has broken into the stadium! It appears that we have . . . a *stage invader*?'

I opened my eyes. All the spotlights had spun round to illuminate this 'invader'. I saw a small creature wearing a familiar silver spacesuit. I saw a pair of curious, friendly brown eyes and a head of fuzzy black hair.

It was swinging across the stadium, flipping from spotlight to spotlight – until he landed on our slice of the stage.

TRACK 20

ARMSTRONG THE STAGE INVADER

'**ARMSTRONG!**' we cheered. 'What are you doing here?'

'Armstrong thought you might be needing these,' the astro-ape said – and we saw then that he was wearing Bash's backpack, and had pulled out a spare pair of drumsticks like a medieval knight unsheathing a sword from its scabbard.

'I don't believe my eye!' Quark Blisterbum said. 'It seems The Earthlings have a *special guest* for their performance. He can't fly a rocket, but let's see if he can *rock it*! Fresh out of hypersleep, it's . . . **ARMSTRONG!**'

Armstrong leaped on to Bash's kick-drum and Bash reached out and grabbed the drumsticks like an Olympic relay runner snatching the baton. Then

Armstrong jumped right over the drum kit and landed on Bash's shoulders.

That's right. Bash was playing the drums on a spaceship with a chimpanzee astronaut on his shoulders.

AWESOME!

The crowd went wild, but the best was yet to come, because as Bash played a fill around his tom-toms with his fresh set of sticks, the astro-ape pulled out his own set of drumsticks from the trusty backpack.

'Armstrong has always wanted to play the drums!' Armstrong said with a twinkle in his big dark eyes.

He spun the sticks around in his long ape fingers, then joined Bash for the most epic double-drummer drum solo I've ever seen.

What am I saying? It's the **ONLY** double-drummer drum solo I've ever seen!

Together, they looked like some strange mutant drum monster with two heads and four arms that were windmilling around the kit so quickly I could barely see them.

BANG! CRASH! THUD! THWACK!

CLACK-CLACK-CLACK!

The fills and rolls were faster than any I'd ever seen before, and I knew if this had been Round One the rock-o-meter would have exploded. But this was Round Two – Rock Till You Drop – and we were back in business with fresh sticks and a special guest.

BRING. IT. ON!

Neila dived into some heavy power chords and I launched back into another chorus.

> The longest, longest, longest song,
> The longest, longest song!
> The longest, longest, longest song,
> This is the longest song . . .

And the stadium joined in, chanting: **'SO LONG!'**

Suddenly there was a pathetic puff of green gas from the Gassy Giants, and a horrid stink that smelled even worse than the time Bash blocked our toilet at home. (It wasn't pretty.)

'And it looks like the Gassy Giants are out of gas!'
Quark chuckled, and Megavolt slammed his burning
fist down on to his red button, sending the trumping
band out of the competition.
'ROUND TWO IS COMPLETE!'
Quark announced as our instruments were beamed
out of our hands and the crowd went wild.

There were only four bands left on the stage. The
Pincers, Pixel Shift, Star Girl – and us! The rest had
joined the other defeated bands in the laser-beam
prison.

'We did it!' Neila cheered, high-fiving Bash and Armstrong.

'That was so awesome when you swung in out of nowhere! You totally saved the show!' Bash said to Armstrong.

'Armstrong found drumsticks in the room. Armstrong couldn't let The Earthlings lose!' replied the astro-ape.

'Yeah, but when you showed up I thought we were going to be disqualified! I didn't think you'd be allowed to join the band. You're not human!' I said.

'He calls Earth home, so he's an *Earthling*. As long as you're from Earth, you can fight for Earth in the battle,' Neila explained.

'Oh! I see. Wait – how do you know that?' I asked Neila. She seemed to suddenly know an awful lot about the rules of the Intergalactic Battle of the Bands.

She froze for a moment, and I'm pretty sure she was about to tell me something . . . something important. But the moment was interrupted by the crowd chanting:

'ECLIPSE! ECLIPSE! ECLIPSE!'

Megavolt gave them what they wanted and blasted his shadow-beam of darkness across the universe, selecting the planets upon which he would soon feast! Megavolt instantly glowed hotter and brighter with just the thought of the planetary picnic he would be devouring.

'MORE!' Megavolt demanded once the planets were dark.

The crowd went wild again, and Quark Blisterbum's voice boomed across the stadium with a surprise announcement.

'You heard His Mightiness. Do *you* want more?' Quark said, and the crowd responded with frenzied screams.

'Then don't go anywhere – because we're heading straight into . . .

LIGHTSPEED ELIMINATION!'

TRACK 21

ROUND THREE: LIGHTSPEED ELIMINATION

The atmosphere in the stadium was electric. (I guess technically there was no atmosphere in the stadium, but you know what I mean.)

'There are just **FOUR** bands remaining: The Pincers, Pixel Shift, Star Girl and The Earthlings!' Quark Blisterbum yelled. 'Our next elimination round is a good old-fashioned, head-to-head, one-on-one battle. The best two bands go through.'

One-on-one! It was like the first round again, only it felt like now the stakes were even higher.

I looked at the other three bands and tried to figure out who I'd rather battle.

Star Girl? She was a master on the guitar. She'd

surely shred us to stardust!

What about Pixel Shift? How could we beat someone who could shape-shift and copy everything we did?

So that only left our first alien friends, The Pincers! Could we really battle Dave, Steve, Beverly and Joyce, and be responsible for their home planet being Megavolt munch? No way!

I didn't want to battle any of them, but we had no choice. It was them or us. Their planet or ours.

Earth was in our shaky hands!

I suddenly thought about home again. About Mum and Dad. My friends. I missed them all. I even missed Mr Lloyd's science lessons. **(I KNOW!)**

Our planet was definitely worth saving.

'Up first, in the blue corner, we have **THE PINCERS!**' Quark Blisterbum announced, and the stage suddenly resembled a wrestling ring, with Dave and his spider-crab-like band huddled in one corner.

'And they'll be fighting, in the red corner – **STAR GIRL!**' Quark continued, and the guitar-wielding alien stepped into the ring like a cowboy in the Wild West, ready to duel.

'**LET'S ROCK!**' Megavolt boomed, and at those words the bands' instruments appeared in the ring.

While The Pincers awkwardly scooped up their guitars and tuned up with their clunky claws, Star Girl wasted no time. She pushed up her glistening green star-shaped glasses and burst into a **SCREAMING** guitar solo that instantly filled the stadium with intergalactic rock awesomeness. Her guitar was like nothing I'd ever seen or heard before. Instead of strings, there were beams of blue light running down the neck like six lightsabers that sparked with energy, and with each fierce strum the guitar changed colour.

'*I want that guitar!*' Neila whispered, gawping like a fish.

'I want those glasses!' I added.

Star Girl tapped furiously, bending notes and plucking melodies that I knew no ordinary Earth guitar could ever make. She slid on her knees, before throwing her guitar in the air, catching it again and playing it behind her head.

'The Pincers don't stand a chance,' I whispered to Bash, who nodded sadly in agreement.

Star Girl finished her performance with an epic leap in the air that seemed to defy gravity as she flung her legs out into the splits before landing with her fist pumping the air triumphantly.

'WOW! What a way to kick off Round Three! Let's see what The Pincers have got to say about that!' Quark Blisterbum said.

There was a sudden stillness in the stadium. All eyes were on the crabby aliens, and my tummy twisted nervously for them as Dave counted in his band of cosmic crustaceans.

Their music wasn't fast and it wasn't rocking, but it had such a happy vibe to it that I was instantly filled with a mellow warmth from top to toe. I felt like I was swinging in a hammock beside the ocean, or dancing at a tropical beach party I wished would never end.

'How are they doing that?' Neila asked, her eyes closed as she swayed happily from side to side.

I took a closer look at Dave, Steve, Joyce and Beverly. The feelers on their heads were all pointing up to the sky . . . and pulsing blue.

'I . . . I think The Pincers' feelers have hypnotic powers?' I whispered dreamily to Bash and Neila. **'I FEEL SO HAPPY!'**

All of a sudden, the stadium was transformed into a holiday far, far away. There were neon palm trees all around us, and the stage was an island of blue sand, surrounded by luminous pink waves that calmly lapped the shore.

'COOOOL, MAN!' said Bash, and I saw that he was wearing a pair of sunglasses and a Hawaiian shirt and was smiling.

'This is wild, dude!' Neila laughed, twirling a bright flower that had appeared in her lucky hat's brim.

'Armstrong feels very happy,' Armstrong said, showing off the glowing flowers on his fuzzy head.

As The Pincers' song came to an end, the hypnotic beach party we were all imagining together started to wear off and we blinked back to reality.

'What in the world just happened?' said Quark, shaking off the daydream. 'Let's see what Star Girl has in response to that . . .'

But Star Girl didn't respond. Star Girl was fast asleep!

'Yet again, I don't believe my eyeball! It seems that The Pincers' melodies have mellowed Star Girl into a deep sleep! The Pincers are through!' Quark Blisterbum declared, and the audience broke into happy cheers.

'WHOA, SHE'S OUT COLD!' Bash said.

'She looks pretty warm to me!' Neila said, as the snoozing Star Girl was carried by a trio of alien roadies to join the other relegated contestants.

'Time to find out who will be joining The Pincers in the next battle! **PIXEL SHIFT** in the blue corner, or The Earthlings in the red?' Quark said, and beckoned us into the wrestling ring.

In the far corner, the three pixelated figures of Pixel Shift were warming up, **GLITCHING** through hundreds of different **DIGITAL FACES AND BODIES**.

'Armstrong is scared,' the space ape said in a small voice. He'd wriggled his body inside Bash's backpack and pulled the zip up so that only his head peeped out. Silence fell in the stadium and all eyes looked at Megavolt.

'Let's **ROCK!**' he roared.

The spotlights hit us. It was our turn first.

'We don't stand a chance!' Neila said. 'Let's face it. We suck!'

'No! We were getting somewhere in that last round. I could feel it!' I replied.

'Not compared to those copycats. We can try and try our hardest, but they'll just do their copying thing and make it better!'

'Well, we've *got* to do our best. The planet is counting on us!' I said, and Neila nodded.

'What song are we playing?' Bash asked.

I glanced at our new bandmate. 'Let's do something different. Let's go for "Loner",' I said.

'Yeah! This is all about you, Armstrong,' Bash told the space chimp, and Armstrong beamed proudly.

'Armstrong, do you want to do the honours?' I asked.

Armstrong took his position on Bash's shoulders again and both drummers held their drumsticks out ready.

'ONE! TWO! THREE! FOUR!' Armstrong shouted, counting us into the song.

'*It's quiet in the universe. No chorus, middle eight or verse*,' I sang. Bash, Armstrong and Neila began to play, all of us trying our very hardest not to suck.

'*Things are only getting worse . . .*' I continued – but in front of us, on the opposite side of the ring,

Pixel Shift were already morphing. Their pixelated faces were transforming into copies of **OUR FACES**, and suddenly the lights shone on us – I mean **THEM!** – as they interrupted our song and took over.

'*It's quiet in the universe. No chorus, middle eight or verse . . .*' the Pixel version of me started singing. He sounded exactly like me . . . only better.

The Pixel copy of Neila was adapting the guitar part too, making it a little more complicated, and the Pixel replication of Bash – complete with Pixel chimpanzee on his Pixel shoulders – was playing a cooler drum part as well.

'Hey!' I shouted. 'Nobody plays our song better than us!'

I took back the song, singing with as much passion and feeling as I could, my fingers trying to find some extra licks on the bass.

TWANG!

Neila hit a bum chord on the dreaded school guitar, which totally clashed with my bass note.

We were surely done for!

Until . . .

TWANG!   **BONK!**   **FLUD!**

The Pixel Neila copied her mistake. Not only did she copy it . . . she made it even worse, twanging her guitar tunelessly.

Thoughts started firing around my brain.

Copy . . .

Better . . .

I felt like the hero in a movie who suddenly figures out exactly how to defeat the bad guy.

'That's it!' I hissed, spinning to face my bandmates. 'We know we can't outplay them. They'll always be better than we are.'

'We know that, genius! So how are we going to beat them? We'll never be good enough!' Bash said.

'Exactly! We'll never be **GOOD** enough, but we definitely know how to play **BADLY!**' I said.

They stared at me for a moment, and then Bash slowly began to smile.

'Of course!' he said. 'Whatever we play, they copy . . .'

'Right! So, if we play our best, they'll always play better . . .' Neila added, seeing where I was going.

'But if we play badly . . .'

'THEY'LL PLAY WORSE!' we all cheered together.

I spun back round and launched into the WORST bass line I could play.

PLONK! THUD! DUFF-DUFF-DUFF!

Armstrong unscrewed the crash cymbals, held one in each hand and smashed them on his head.

CRASH! CRASH!

Bash started mis-hitting the drums, clicking the metal rims of the kit.

CLICK-CLACK! CLICK-CLACK!

And Neila let rip on that school guitar, totally embracing its awfulness.

BOING! TWANG! GONG! DOING!

'The Earthlings seem to have lost the plot!' uttered

Quark Blisterbum. 'Are they giving up? I think we have a clear winner . . .'

But before Megavolt could call victory, Pixel Shift glitched and flickered as they copied the new information and started replicating us.

PLONK!
   CRASH!
      CLICK-CLACK!
        BOING! TWANG!

It sounded bad! Just like us – only worse.

WAY WORSE!

'I don't believe my ears! This is the worst sound I've ever heard in the entire universe!' cried Quark, flinging his webbed hands over his alien ears.

The crowd started booing and hissing, throwing their space snacks at the stage.

'MAKE IT STOP! MAKE IT STOP!
        MAKE IT STOP!'   they chanted.

But Pixel Shift didn't stop. They just got worse and worse, until . . .

BOOM!

A mighty sound echoed around the stadium as Megavolt slammed his plasma fist on the arm of his throne, calling for silence.

'PIXEL SHIFT . . . LOSE!' Megavolt growled.

The stadium exploded with applause, and Pixel Shift digitized back to their original pixelated form.

'We did it!' Bash cheered.

'We sucked!' Neila whooped.

'Well, when it comes to playing badly, we're the best!' I joked as we all leaped around in celebration.

Being the worst band in the world had got us through another round.

The crowd started chanting: '**ECLIPSE! ECLIPSE! ECLIPSE!**' And Megavolt gave them exactly what they wanted. His black-hole energy beam of shadowy darkness blasted out of the Space Stadium and plunged Star Girl's star system – Shred, circled by guitar-string rings – and Pixel Shift's planet – the pixelated Digitropolis – into total darkness. He admired them on the enormous screens around the stadium for a moment, staring at them the way Dad stares at the fish and chips menu at Fred's back on Earth.

'**MORE!**' Megavolt demanded.

The crowd went wild.

'You heard His Rockiness,' announced Quark. 'Time for the last elimination round. The **SEMI-FINAL!** This will decide who will be facing Megavolt.'

Suddenly I realized what was coming. My heart sank in my chest.

'IT'S THE PINCERS VERSUS THE EARTHLINGS!'

TRACK 22

THE SEMI-FINAL

There were just two bands left on stage. The Pincers and us.

I looked across the stadium at Dave, Steve, Beverly and Joyce. They looked back sadly.

'We don't stand a chance, do we?' Neila sighed.

'Against their hypnotic powers? Nope!' I confirmed.

'I guess this is it, then. The end of the world,' Bash added.

'Armstrong is sad,' Armstrong piped up as Quark Blisterbum stepped into a spotlight centre stage.

'The winner of the semi-final will be decided by an audience vote!' Quark said, and the audience responded with an **'OOOOOOOOOOH!'**

'Aliens of the audience, you'll each find a keypad on your seat. Please put your fingers, claws, suckers, tentacles, or whatever pointy bits you might have, on your keypads, and get ready to vote for the band you wish to be *eliminated*. Remember, this isn't *vote to save*. This is *vote to ECLIPSE*!'

'ENOUGH TALKING. MEGAVOLT HUNGRY. TIME TO ROCK!' Megavolt growled.

'Quite right, Your Rockiness. Performing first is . . .'

I gulped. *Please not us. Please not us. Please not us.*

'THE EARTHLINGS!'

The blinding spotlights hit us instantly and we had no choice but to play.

'Let's do "The Greatest Band in the Universe" again, OK?' I said, and my bandmates nodded.

'ONE! TWO! THREE! FOUR!' Bash yelled, and he and Armstrong smashed around the kit.

I joined in, plodding along on the bass line while Neila entered what looked like a wrestling match with the disastrous school guitar, a wrestling match she was losing, by the sound of it. The noise we were making was so bad it was almost impressive. The guitar sounded like a choir of six wailing cats all miaowing out of tune at the same time, while the drums sounded like an elephant stomping on a tin roof. And my bass sounded like a floppy plastic bag flapping around on a windy day . . .

FLOP! FLAP! FLURP!

If I'd thought we were starting to get a little better before, I saw now that the pressure of this round was really getting to us. We were worse than we'd ever been. We sounded like Dad's imaginary car crash in the garage again. If we had been on Earth, Dad would definitely have called the police.

At least The Pincers would win, I told myself. At least our friends would still have the chance to get back to their home planet, even if we wouldn't.

It wasn't long before the audience started booing us.

'You suck!'

'Get off the stage!'

'This isn't music – this is torture!'

'MAKE IT STOP!'

I could barely hear what we were playing over their heckles, and our song crashed to a disastrous, wailing, stomping, flappy ending.

'Well, I think we're all pleased that's over,' Quark Blisterbum said, laughing. 'Let's see if the next band can do a little better than that! Give it up for The Pincers!'

The spotlights swung over to Dave, Steve, Beverly and Joyce, who faced us.

But they didn't start playing.

'I said, **THE PINCERS!**' Quark repeated. His voice echoed across the silent stadium as he looked around awkwardly.

But still The Pincers didn't play.

'We cannot battle,' Dave announced, placing his guitar on the stage.

The crowd started murmuring excitedly as the rest of The Pincers followed their leader in laying down their instruments, as if in surrender.

'We owe The Earthlings a *life debt*,' Dave revealed, sending gasps around the crowd. 'We are sworn to protect them, and therefore it is forbidden for us to battle against them.' Dave nodded at us.

'Earthlings, is this true?' Quark asked.

'Dave, don't do this!' I hissed at our friend. 'At least give yourselves a chance to save your planet. **YOU OWE IT TO THEM!**'

'We would not have made it this far without you, Earthlings,' Dave said, a note of proud sadness in his crabby eyes. 'Now we must repay the debt. Please, show your marks.'

We looked at each other, unsure.

'Do it, Earthlings!' urged Beverly.

Reluctantly, we pulled back our sleeves to reveal the pincer-shaped marks on our arms. The crowd gasped.

'It is true! The Pincers must forfeit the match!' Quark bellowed.

'No, wait! There must be another way!' I shouted.

'I wish there was, but this is the only way,' said Dave.

Megavolt suddenly rose to his feet, glowing with fury.

'PLAY!' he exploded.

'We cannot,' replied Dave bravely.

'If you do not play, I will eclipse your planet!' Megavolt roared with rage.

Dave and the other Pincers all remained silent.

'So be it!' Megavolt growled. He slammed his fist on to the shadow beam. We could barely watch as the beam blasted across the universe to suck every speck of light out of Crustacea.

It was done. The Pincers had put their own planet on the menu for Megavolt's end-of-battle banquet, and Earth had been saved.

I felt a tingle on my arm, and saw the pincer tattoo flicker for a second before disappearing. It was gone – although I knew that one day, when I was old enough, I'd have that tattoo again, but for real! I looked over at The Pincers, a huge lump in my throat – no matter what happened, we'd always remember their friendship – and they waved back as they left the stage.

'Well, folks, that was an unexpected twist to the

elimination round, but you know what that means . . .'
Quark started leaping around on the spot with so
much excitement he could have been Buxy's fourth
member as he revealed:

'THE EARTHLINGS
ARE THE CHAMPIONS!'

Fireworks exploded all around us and the crowd
went wild. A huge hologram of Planet Earth
appeared in the centre of the stadium, its blues and
greens vivid compared to the eclipsed planets.

'Out of sixteen bands from across the universe,
only one would make it through. Only one would
save their planet. Only one would return home! That
one band is you!' Quark beamed at us.

'We . . . we won? We get to go home?' Bash gasped.

'Yes! Yes! Yes! You are the champions and in just a

few moments you will be beamed back across the universe, bending the laws of space and time to take you to that beautiful planet of yours, to the exact moment you left, like nothing ever happened!'

'Armstrong too?' Armstrong said hopefully.

'Of course! Of course!' Quark smiled.

'But what about *them*? The other bands?' I asked. But I knew the answer. Megavolt was already salivating hot solar flares from his lips as he prepared to consume fifteen eclipsed planets.

'I'm afraid Megavolt will now pull their planets across the universe, harnessing the gravity of the black hole to crush them into bite-sized balls for his feast, until all that's left of them are memories!' Quark declared. '*Unless*, that is, you decide to . . .

GRAVITY GAMBLE!'

There was a sudden hush around the stadium as if someone had muted the sound.

'Don't risk it! Go home. Save your planet!' Dave shouted.

'SILENCE!' demanded Megavolt. 'I'm hungry. Make your choice.'

'If you choose to Gravity Gamble, you will have to face Megavolt in the Grand Final. Winner takes all,' Quark explained. 'If you win, the defeated bands' planets will be *un-eclipsed* and everyone, including you, will return safely home! You will forever be known as The Greatest Band in the Universe.'

'But if we lose?' Neila asked.

'If you lose, then Earth along with all the other planets will belong to Megavolt and will be destroyed!' Quark said matter-of-factly, as if the end of the world was no big deal.

'GRAVITY GAMBLE! GRAVITY GAMBLE! GRAVITY GAMBLE!' chanted the crowd as I turned to look at Bash. Then Neila. And finally Armstrong. Each of them simply nodded at me. We didn't need to say anything. We all knew what we had to do.

'We've made our choice,' I announced. 'Why save one world when you can save them all? We choose to **GRAVITY GAMBLE!**'

There was a deafening roar of applause around the stadium.

'I don't believe my noise receptors! The Earthlings are risking everything! We'll see if they have what it takes tomorrow night in the ultimate Grand Final!'

All around us, the massive screens flashed:

MEGAVOLT VERSUS
THE EARTHLINGS!

TRACK 23

BACK IN THE DRESSING ROOM

After the show, we were way too tired for the chaos of Catering, which was crammed with backstage crew trying to get their claws (literally!) on Chef Garble's now legendary peet-sa.

'I'm afraid we're all out of peet-sa,' Garble told us apologetically. 'But I've made you another classic Earth dish instead. Chee spurgas!'

'Chee spurgas?' Bash said, screwing up his face.

Garble pressed a button and as a hovering tray full of his creations floated across the busy room we realized exactly what *chee spurgas* were.

'Cheeseburgers!' we cheered.

We dived to take one of the four whopping great big whoppers.

CRASH!

I guess Neila was hungrier than me and Bash, as she crashed right into Garble, sending the hover-tray of burgers hurtling through air before any of us could get our hands on one.

SPLAT! SPLOSH! SPLISH! SPLODGE!

All over the spaceship floor.

'Sorry!' Neila shrugged, helping Garble to his feet, who dusted himself off and promised to make some more chee spurgas right away. For now, we followed Beep-Bop to our fake-Earth dressing room in hungry silence.

'Wake Armstrong up for the next round!' Armstrong said with a yawn as he swung himself inside his hypersleep pod, which kept him as fresh as the day he launched into space.

'Don't worry, we will. You're part of the band now!' said Bash, tucking the astro-ape into his refrigerated bed and closing the door. It sealed with a hiss and the blink of a green light.

We climbed into our triple bunk beds, and I was so tired I didn't even try to fight for the top one. I just dived into the middle bunk and within minutes I heard Bash snoring above me. Neila was silently snoozing below.

But, as tired as I was, I couldn't sleep. I just stared out of the enormous window at the stars and galaxies, billions of them twinkling and shining across the universe. Somewhere out there was our home, Earth. So teeny that it was impossible for me to see, but I knew it was there, drifting through space.

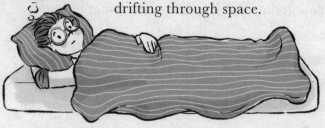

I imagined for a moment what it would be like to see our planet consumed by a supermassive Megavolt, so large he could swallow it whole.

Everything that had ever happened, everything that is happening right now – or could happen in the future – all gone in one giant gulp! As I stared at

Spectra, the unthinkably enormous black hole, I realized that Earth is so tiny compared to everything else in this universe, yet somehow still so important.

Still worth saving.

Worth fighting for.

I was just starting to drift into a dream when I heard the smooth sound of our dressing-room door sliding open.

SWISH!

'Who's there?' I whispered.

There was no reply.

'Armstrong? Is that you?' I hissed.

There was still nothing, and I could see the green light of his freeze pod blinking. That meant it couldn't have been Armstrong who had made the noise.

'Bash, did you hear that?' I whispered.

Bash replied with a loud snore, the kind he makes when he's in the deepest of sleeps. I knew it would take a direct hit from an asteroid to wake him!

'Neila, did *you* hear it?' I said, hanging my head over the side of my bunk to see if she was awake.

NEILA'S BED WAS EMPTY!

'Neila?' I whispered as I climbed out of my bunk and crept across the dressing room in the dark.

There was still no reply. And I was about to find out why . . .

The star-shaped door to our dressing room was open, and from out in the corridor I heard footsteps getting quieter, as though someone was hurrying away. I quickly poked my head out to see who it was and, to my surprise, I saw Neila, creeping off down the unlit corridor, walking like someone who doesn't want to be followed.

I glanced up and down the corridor to check that no one else had seen her. Beep-Bop had said if anyone was caught leaving their dressing rooms at night they would be **DISQUALIFIED!**

Why would Neila risk Planet Earth being destroyed? It had to be serious. Was she in trouble? Where was she sneaking to on board a spaceship in the middle of the night?

There was only one way to find out. I did what anyone else would do. I followed her, of course!

I wondered if she was hungry and was going to see if Garble had cooked up any more chee spurgas yet, but as I followed her through the quiet corridors she tippy-toed straight past the door to Catering.

So I did too.

Then she crept through the backstage area, staying in the shadows, ducking behind flight cases and crawling underneath the stage as roadies and crew worked through the night to get the stadium ready for tomorrow's battle.

It wasn't long until we were in the depths of Megavolt's ship, and Neila was creeping faster and faster as if she was on a secret mission – until she stopped outside a shiny golden door with words etched into its smooth metallic surface.

I screwed up my eyes and tried to read them in the dim light.

'*House of Boos?*' I whispered to myself. What on earth could be kept in there?

Neila paused for a moment and I silently crept closer, like a ninja. Like a space ninja. Like a *ninjastronaut*.

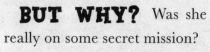

She reached into her pocket and pulled out a glowing key card.

My mind suddenly flashed back and I remembered that exact key card in Garble's hand as he told us: *'I'm the only one Megavolt trusts with a key that opens every door!'*

But how was this possible? Why did Neila have Garble's key card and how had she got it?

My mind zoomed back again to the tray of chee spurgas flying through the air earlier that day, when *Neila crashed into Garble.* She must have stolen his key card from him as she helped him to his feet!

BUT WHY? Was she really on some secret mission?

If I wanted to find out the truth, I had to stay quiet and keep following her.

Neila held the glowing key card up to a panel on the door and – **SWISH!** – the door slid open. I had to duck as Neila glanced back to check she wasn't being followed before stepping into this *House of Boos*.

Suddenly the door started swishing shut. If I wanted to get to the bottom of this mystery, I was on the wrong side of it! I dashed out of the shadows and through the door like an awesome action hero, just in time for it to close behind me.

I was **IN!**

TRACK 24

THE HOUSE OF BOOS

The House of Boos was like a giant, cavernous warehouse, only more outer-spacey. It's how I imagine our local DIY store that Dad loves so much will look in a hundred years.

There were hundreds of aisles with huge containers stacked on top of each other, right up to the ceiling. Each one had the same sparking red laser-beam bars as the prison that had held the eliminated bands back in the stadium. It made me think that Megavolt *really* didn't want anyone getting inside these things! What was also weird was what sounded like a booing crowd. I guess this was why it was called the House of Boos . . .

CLINK!

A noise up ahead distracted me from the booing. I could see Neila further along the aisle, peering through the red lasers as though she was looking for something.

'Hello?' she whispered.

My brain hurt, even more than when I was in Mrs Spearing's maths class, as I stood there trying to make sense of what was happening. So many questions bounced around my head. Who was Neila looking for? Why were they in this House of Boos? And most importantly . . . **WHAT WAS THAT THING TOUCHING MY LEG?!**

I looked down and saw a long, veiny vine-like arm reaching through the laser bars of the cage next to me. It had wrapped itself round my calf.

Megavolt wasn't trying to stop things getting IN these cages, I realized – he was trying to stop things getting **OUT!**

'**AAARGGHHHH!**' I yelped. 'Get it off me!'

My cover was blown! Neila came running to my rescue, grabbing the vine-like arm and trying to untangle the creature's grip on my leg.

'Get it off!' I screamed, but the more I shook and wriggled, the tighter it curled.

'Hold still!' Neila shouted, and she reached up and touched the sides of her head with the tips of her middle fingers.

'What are you doing? Get it off, Neila!' I squealed.

'Just be quiet and let me concentrate!' she snapped, and frowned as if she was focusing on a super-difficult question.

Suddenly her eyes started to glow green.

'Whoa . . .' I whispered in disbelief.

Then, within the shadows of the cage, I saw another pair of eyes light up the same vivid green colour. Neila waved her arm and the creature loosened its veiny vine from round my leg and retracted it through the laser bars.

Neila's eyes dimmed, and I was free.

'WHAT JUST HAPPENED?'

I yelled.

'You're welcome!' Neila replied sarcastically.

She helped me to my feet. We both stood and looked at each other for a moment.

'Seriously,' I said. 'What is going on?'

Neila sighed.

'I was at home one night, about to go to bed, when I saw something falling out of the sky,' she explained. 'It crashed in the woods. I grabbed my torch, went to take a closer look, and found a . . .'

'A meteorite?' I guessed.

'A spaceship!' Neila whispered.

Before we'd been beamed up into space, I'd never have believed Neila. I'd have thought she'd been listening to too many of Bash's stories. Now, though, I knew that we really were not alone in the universe. Neila might just be telling the truth.

'So what did you do?' I replied.

'I touched it. And then I got scared, and ran

home . . . but the next morning I discovered that I had these . . . *powers*,' she said, nervously adjusting her lucky hat.

'No way! I have **SO** many questions! What kind of powers? Why didn't you tell us? When did this happen?' I asked.

'About a year ago,' Neila said.

Bash and Armstrong tumbled out of the shadows where they'd been hiding.

'*A year ago?*' Bash blurted.

'I thought you were in bed! What are you doing here?' I asked.

'**US?** We're following **YOU!** What are *you* doing here?' Bash threw back at me.

'**ME?** I was following **HER!**' I said, pointing to Neila.

'So I *did* see a UFO land in the woods last year!' Bash said. 'I told you, didn't I, George? I knew I should have gone looking for it. Then I would have got awesome space superpowers too!'

'Are you angry at me for keeping it secret?' Neila asked nervously.

Bash and I looked at each other and started laughing.

'*Angry?*' I said. 'Our best friend has space superpowers! This is the coolest day ever!'

'So, what kind of things can you do? Is it like *the Force?*' Bash grinned like an excited puppy.

'It's nothing like the Force, Bash. You watch too many movies,' Neila said, rolling her eyes.

'Can you see through walls? Can you glow in the dark? Can you read minds? What number am I thinking of?' Bash asked.

'No! It's not that kind of power!' Neila protested.

'Well, if you can't do any of those things, it sounds like a pretty rubbish superpower to me . . .' Bash teased.

Neila took the bait.

Suddenly her eyes started glowing green again, and I had the overwhelming desire to . . . *dance!*

My arms started flapping around under Neila's control,

and I couldn't stop myself from busting out the robot, followed by the worm.

'Wait – what's happening? Are *you* doing this?' I said as I body-popped around.

'Yep!' Neila said proudly.

'*This* is your superpower? You can make people do silly dances?'

'No! Not just dance.' She grinned mischievously.

My right hand started rising towards my face and my finger stuffed itself . . . up my nose. Then my left hand grabbed the back of my pants and I gave myself an atomic wedgie!

'Oof!' I said.

Bash and Armstrong fell to the floor laughing.

'Your turn!' Neila sang, and with her palms pointing at the three of us, she raised her arms towards the ceiling. Our feet suddenly left the ground.

'**ARGH!** Put me down! Put me down!' Bash cried as Neila levitated us around the room.

'OK, if you say so!'

And, with that, she let us go.

'That was **AWESOME!**' I cheered.

Armstrong smiled. 'Armstrong likes flying!'

'You totally have *the Force*!' Bash said, rubbing his sore bum.

Once I'd dusted myself off and readjusted my underwear, I glanced around and suddenly remembered where we were – the House of Boos.

'Neila, what are you down here for?' I whispered. 'I know you took Garble's key card to get inside. But why?'

'Because –'

But before Neila could finish there was a noise from somewhere further along the dark aisle. A voice.

'HELLO? IS SOMEONE THERE?' the voice called.

Neila's eyes suddenly **BLAZED** brighter than ever, and she dashed down the aisle as if she was in the final sprint on Sports Day.

We all followed her, **TWISTING** and **TURNING** through the dark aisles, following the voice calling to us. Neila didn't stop until she'd reached a cage with four aliens inside.

They looked almost human, except for a single antenna sticking out of their heads. Two of them rushed to the laser-beam bars excitedly.

'Er, hi! I'm George.' I waved. 'These are my friends, Neila, Bash and Armstrong. We're all from Earth.'

'All of you?' the creatures replied, looking a little confused.

'Oh, yeah, he's a chimp and we're human. We're kind of different on our planet, but we're all Earthlings,' I explained.

'Well, hello, Earthlings,' the aliens in the cage said.

'You may call me Annavoig,' said one of them.

'And I'm Mot,' said another.

'Pleased to meet you, *Annavoig* and *Mot*,' I said, trying my best to pronounce their unusual names.

'Are you in a band too? Is that why you're in this House of Boos?' Bash asked.

The alien named Mot sighed, and began telling us a story that was so

MIND-BOGGLINGLY OUT OF THIS WORLD

that it could easily have been another one of Bash's comics . . .

ROCKSTAR WARS: VOL. 2

Still in a distant world and a distant time, in the Anadrome galaxy on a planet named Tenalp, there was a band called DAB and they were the WORST band on the entire planet!

One day, DAB were rocking out when — BOOM! They were beamed aboard the Space Stadium and forced to enter Megavolt's Intergalactic Battle of the Bands. 'I will eat the losers' planet for lunch! Mwah-ha-ha!' Megavolt laughed. 'But we suck!' Mot said. 'Yeah, we ALL suck!' protested all the other bands.

'You mean, I beamed up all the WORST bands in the universe? What a happy coincidence . . .' Megavolt cackled.

So the AWFUL band tried their hardest, but they really did suck!

Meanwhile, back on
Planet Tenalp . . .

Annavoig and Mot's child
was watching their mum
and dad's terrible band
battle on the TV.

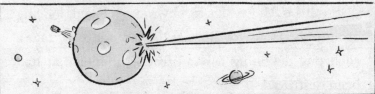

'They're not going to make it!' they cried. So, before Megavolt ZAPPED
Planet Tenalp and ate it, the child climbed into an escape pod and
blasted into space . . . JUST IN TIME!

Back on the SPACE STADIUM . . .

'Our planet is gone!' Annavoig cried.

'Yeah! Where are we going to live?'
Mot wailed.

'You will all live HERE!'
Megavolt laughed.

He put all the awful bands in
cages and locked them in his
House of Boos . . . FOREVER!

To be continued . . .

Maybe . . .

TRACK 25

THERE IS A WAY

'So this is Megavolt's trophy room?' I said, looking around the House of Boos at the thousands of cages, each one detaining a band from a planet that had been destroyed.

'Yes, this is where we live now. Even if we weren't trapped in this place, we have no planet to return to. We are stranded,' Mot said sadly.

'And your child managed to escape Tenalp before it was destroyed?' I asked.

'Yes,' Annavoig said with a slight smile.

'How do you know?' Bash asked.

The two aliens looked at each other with love in their twinkling green eyes.

'We just know. We can *feel* it,' they said.

'**WHOA, THAT'S COOL!** I wish I had that power, then I'd be able to *feel* when my mum and dad are coming upstairs to check on me when

I'm drumming on my pillow instead of going to bed,' Bash said.

Now, I'm no hero, but looking at these poor planetless aliens who had lost their kid made me want to do something.

'When we defeat Megavolt and win this battle, I promise we'll set you free and help you find your family,' I said.

Annavoig and Mot smiled.

'Ah, so you're a band too?' Mot asked.

'Yes! We are The Earthlings. We are here to save Planet Earth!' Armstrong told them proudly.

But, as he said that, I remembered what Mot had said about Megavolt only beaming up the **WORST** bands from around the universe. I remembered what Dave had told me at the very start of the contest too: that no one had ever beaten Megavolt.

'If everything you've said is true, then it's all a fix. It's **ALWAYS A FIX**. We'll never win! No one will,' I realized.

'Correct, Earthling. Every one of us in here

represents the very worst music from our home planets,' Annavoig said.

'It's true. We're awful on our planet!' said the pink furred lead singer of the Furry Wurzlets from a cage above.

'Same here. We totally **SUCK!**' bubbled Slimeblob and Gloop.

'Affirmative. We are also the worst band on Corrodia,' droned 8-TRAX, and I saw that all the bands we'd seen knocked out of the competition were here in cages. Pixel Shift, Buxy, Michael Doublé – everyone. Even our friends The Pincers were here, gripping the bars of their cage with their giant claws and peering out at us sadly.

'But you're all **AWESOME** bands!' Bash said.

'Not where we come from. Oh no, we are very bad indeed,' Dave said, sighing.

'So we really *are* the worst band on Planet Earth!' I huffed, slumping to the floor and feeling totally defeated.

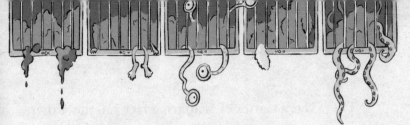

After all that hard work in our garage, all the scribbled lyrics in this book of rock, it turns out we're just another rubbish band with a dream that will never come true.

Finally I understood all that booing. It was Megavolt's cruel reminder to everyone in here that they really were the worst bands in the universe.

'I'm sorry, young human, but it's impossible to win. Megavolt makes the rules. It's his show,' Mot said. 'Megavolt is always the champion.'

'Unless the legend is true . . .' spoke a deep voice from the shadows of one of the cages above.

It was Dark Matter, the mysterious opera-singing alien.

'What legend?' Neila asked.

'Don't listen to them, Earthling friends. It's just a rumour,' said Dave.

'My sensors suggest the legend is true!' added 8-TRAX.

'*What legend?*' I demanded.

There was a clatter of scattering feet and the slither of tentacles as hundreds of aliens stepped up to the bars of their prisons to hear this mysterious legend told.

Dark Matter emerged slowly from the darkness, their face bathed in the deep-red glow of their laser prison.

'Legend has it that at the end of the universe, on the edge of a vast black hole, there is an object. Whoever discovers this object will be worthy of harnessing the power of **UNLIMITED MUSICAL POTENTIAL**,' Dark Matter intoned.

'*Unlimited musical potential?* What does that even mean?' I asked.

'It means that whoever finds that mythical object will be given the power to **ROCK HARDER, FASTER AND LOUDER** than anyone in the universe!' Slimeblob and Gloop squelched.

'You would have the power of musical awesomeness, dude,' added Star Girl.

'The power to defeat Megavolt, once and for all,'

Dark Matter confirmed.

'But how do we get to the edge of a black hole at the end of the universe?' Neila asked.

'You are already there,' Dark Matter said.

'*Spectra!*' I gasped, remembering the enormous black hole we could see from our dressing-room window.

Dark Matter nodded.

'So let's go and get this object, whatever it is!' Bash said.

Dave and the other Pincers scoffed.

'It is impossible. First, you would need to steal one of Megavolt's starships, which are kept locked inside the launch bay,' said Beverly.

We all slumped. *Impossible.*

'Wait! I've got a key that opens **ANY** door!' Neila squeaked, pulling out Garble's glowing key card.

'**YES!**' I cheered.

'Not so fast. You'd also need someone who knows how to pilot a starship,' one of the Furry Wurzlets said.

We slumped again.

Totally impossible.

'Ooh-ooh-ooh! Me! Me! Me! Armstrong knows how to fly space rockets! Armstrong trained for years!' Armstrong shrieked, leaping around excitedly and pointing at his astronaut suit.

Excited whispers hissed all around the House of Boos as the defeated aliens looked at each other.

'Could it be true?'

'Could this be the band that finally defeats Megavolt?'

'They'll never find it . . .'

'This is what we've been waiting for!'

'If this mysterious object exists, it could be our only shot at defeating Megavolt and saving our planet. We have a **KEY**. We have a **PILOT**. What do you say, Earthlings?' I said to my bandmates.

Neila suddenly looked nervous, hiding her eyes behind her tuft of fringe.

'I don't know if I can do it!' she said, trembling.

'Neila, if you have a chance to save Earth, you must give it everything you have,' Annavoig said.

'But what if I can't? What if I let the whole planet down?' Neila sniffed.

'It is better to try and fail than to fail to try,' Mot said, like some sort of wise alien wizard. It sounded a bit like something Max Riff might say, and I found myself nodding respectfully.

My bandmates glanced at each other anxiously, but there was now a little twinkle in their eyes that wasn't there before. A twinkle of excitement. A twinkle of hope!

'All those in favour of stealing a starship, finding a mysterious object on the edge of a black hole, getting musical superpowers and saving the world, say: **LET'S ROCK!**' I said, and Bash, Neila and Armstrong replied together:

'LET'S ROCK!'

TRACK 26

NO TIME TO LOSE!

We said our goodbyes to the aliens in the House of Boos, darted back through the golden door and made our way through the shadows into the backstage world of the Space Stadium.

This wasn't a competition any more. It was a top-secret space mission to save the world. We weren't just a band – we were space-warriors from Earth out to defeat Megavolt!

'How do we find the launch bay?' I whispered.

'Over there!' Neila said, spotting a handy sign on the opposite side of the stadium that said:

> **LAUNCH BAY – THIS WAY!**

I've no idea how, but it seemed that the translation passes could even translate the signs for us. It was like magic – I looked at the symbols and somehow knew what they said!

'Well, that was easy!' Bash smiled.

'Yeah, but if anyone sees us out of our dressing room, we'll be disqualified,' I reminded my bandmates as we all hid behind a stack of empty flight cases.

By now, there were alien roadies at work all over the place, rolling equipment from one side of the stadium to the other and getting the venue ready for the final battle.

'How are The Earthlings going to sneak all the way over there without being seen?' Armstrong asked, just as we had to duck for cover while a four-armed roadie heaved a heavy flight case past our shadowy hiding place.

'I've got it! We do the *Max Riff B-stage illusion*!' I said excitedly.

'The Max Riff *what*-stage illusion?' Neila said, screwing up her face.

'When Max Riff plays live, he always has **TWO** stages. The main stage, where he plays most of the show, and then a secret B stage right in the middle of the stadium.'

'OK, so what's that got to do with us secretly getting to the launch bay over there?' Bash asked.

'Well, Max Riff doesn't just casually walk to the B stage. He's a rock star, so he appears there as if he's been transported by rock magic!' I explained.

'Great. Just one problem, George. We don't have rock magic!' Bash said.

'No, but the *Max Riff Backstage Tour* documentary revealed how he really gets to the B stage.' I grinned. 'Any guesses?'

'A secret tunnel under the stadium?' Neila guessed.

'Nope!'

'He abseils down from the ceiling under a veil of darkness?' Bash said.

'Nope! All right, I'll tell you! It's **So** simple.'

I opened my book of rock and drew them this handy diagram:

'When the lights go black, Max Riff climbs inside an ordinary flight case and his stage roadies wheel

him through the crowd, right past his screaming fans, all the way to the B stage. There's always loads of equipment being wheeled around a stadium so no one ever guesses that there's a superstar hiding inside!' I explained – and I reached round and clicked open the latch of the flight case we were hiding behind.

'So you want us to just climb inside this dark box?' Bash asked hesitantly.

'Yep!'

'But how do you know one of these roadies will wheel us to the launch bay? We could end up anywhere on the ship!' Neila said.

'Good point,' I replied, ripping a page from my book of rock. I scribbled **DELIVER TO LAUNCH BAY** on it and placed it on top of the flight case where no roadie could fail to spot it. Then we all bundled inside and shut the door.

'It's darker than a black hole in here!' Bash said.

'Ow, whose foot is that?' Neila asked.

'Not mine!' I replied. 'Ew, what's that smell?'

'Armstrong is sorry.'

Neila gagged. 'Gross!'

'I'm in space, trying to save the world, trapped in a dark box with a farting astronaut chimp. My life is so weird,' Bash said while pinching his nose.

'Shhhh, someone's coming!' I whispered.

Outside, I heard the footsteps of the four-armed roadie returning. I could hear him breathing outside, just inches away.

'*Launch bay*,' he grumbled, reading my note, then . . .

WHOOOSH!

We were off! The four of us secretly squished inside desperately tried to stay silent as we were whizzed across the stadium. We spun and swayed, bumped and bashed, twisted and turned, all in total darkness like a really, really bad rollercoaster.

'I want to get off!' Neila whispered.

'I feel sick!' Bash gulped.

'Faster! *WHEEEEEE!*' laughed Armstrong, clearly enjoying the ride.

'Shhh, we're nearly there!' I said as the flight case started to slow down.

'Here we go. *Launch bay*,' grumbled our roadie driver as we came to a halt and I listened to his heavy footsteps trudge away.

'Armstrong, is that your bum again?' Bash whispered.

'Sorry, Armstrong gets gassy when Armstrong's excited!' the stinky ape confessed.

CLICK!

I opened the flight-case lid and felt warm air that smelled like an ape's backside rush past as we all bundled out into a heap on the floor, right outside the launch-bay door. Neila tapped Chef Garble's master key card on the pad and the door swished open, revealing a giant hangar filled with row upon row of shimmering starships.

Bash beamed. 'This is the best day of my life.'

Armstrong scampered over to the nearest one, leaped up to the door and hit a large button, which made the door hiss open. We climbed aboard, strapping ourselves into the cockpit with Armstrong in the pilot's seat.

'I'll be **CO-PILOT**,' Bash said, pushing past me and climbing into the seat next to Armstrong.

'Oooh, has the small human flown a starship before?' Armstrong asked.

'Not quite, but I've read enough sci-fi to know what I'm doing. Shall we start the pre-space-flight checks?' Bash said knowingly.

'Checks?' Armstrong laughed. 'There is no time for checks! **HIT IT!**'

And, with that, our primate pilot slammed a lever forward, igniting the thrusters and launching our starship into the air.

'Armstrong has missed flying! Yahoo!' Armstrong cheered as we sped through the airlock doors and into outer space.

'I miss the flight case!' Bash screamed as Armstrong spun the starship upside down and we all held on for dear life.

'FULL SPEED TO SPECTRA!' I shouted.

'Affirmative, Captain!' Armstrong said as we zoomed away from the Space Stadium and towards the looming black hole.

TRACK 27

THE MYSTERIOUS OBJECT

We raced across the galaxy as fast as we could, with Armstrong guiding our ship through asteroid fields and wearing a toothy smile as big as a crescent moon.

Could we really make it to this mysterious object, get these legendary musical powers and return in time for the final?

There was only one way to find out.

Suddenly the cockpit started getting **DARKER** . . . and **DARKER** . . . and **DARKER** as we flew closer to the black hole that Spectra had left behind.

But it wasn't just black. It was somehow darker than black. It was like looking directly at midnight with your eyes closed while wearing a blindfold. It was as if light had never existed at all.

But on the very edge of that darkness was a tiny

speck of light, shimmering like a little diamond that wanted to be found.

'That's it!' Neila said. 'The mysterious object!'

'How can you be sure?' I asked.

Without warning, the radar on board our starship started beeping.

'**MYSTERIOUS OBJECT DETECTED**,' the starship's flight computer announced.

'Told you!' Neila said with a grin.

Armstrong slammed down on the forward thrusters and, as we zoomed towards it, the little bright dot got bigger . . . and bigger . . . and **BIGGER**.

'**MYSTERIOUS OBJECT APPROACHING**,' the flight computer announced.

'It's an abandoned rocket!' Bash whispered excitedly.

'Maybe the mysterious object is on board?' Neila wondered.

'What in the galaxy could it be?' I added, staring at the battered old rocket ship that was now filling our starship's windscreen.

'Armstrong knows exactly what is on board that

rocket,' our chimpanzee pilot said, his dark eyes fixed ahead as if he'd seen a ghost.

'How could you possibly know?' I asked.

'Because that is not just any rocket. That is *Armstrong's* rocket!' Armstrong said, and we all stared as huge red letters came into view on the side of the ship, spelling out its name:

MINERVA 7.

I grabbed my book of rock and quickly flicked to the sketch I'd done in Mr Lloyd's class just a few days ago, although now it felt like a distant dream. I held my doodle up to the windscreen, and it was identical.

It was the *Minerva 7* all right.

'Armstrong will take us aboard,' said our pilot.

We held on tight as Armstrong steered our starship right up to the *Minerva 7*, and we docked beside the airlock. Armstrong hit a series of buttons and levers and the airlock opened with a hiss of white gas, and the four of us floated aboard.

It was silent and eerie inside the gigantic abandoned spacecraft, and I suddenly felt as if I was a deep-sea diver exploring a shipwreck on the ocean floor. Neila,

Bash and I drew a little closer together.

'Follow Armstrong. Armstrong will take you to the *mysterious object*,' Armstrong said.

We followed our ape guide through the guts of his ancient ghost ship, until he came to a sudden stop in the **CARGO BAY**.

Dim lights flickered on as we entered this cavernous section of the ship. It was totally empty except for a strange black box floating in the centre of the room.

'There it is,' Armstrong whispered with wide, wondering eyes, pointing to the strange object.

'There *what* is?' Bash asked.

'The object containing the power of musical awesomeness,' Armstrong said in awe.

We floated over to the small box and Bash gave it an experimental poke.

'What does it do? How do we get the powers out?' he said.

'Wait a minute,' I said. My mind was racing back to Mr Lloyd's science lesson and what he'd told us about the *Minerva 7*. 'This isn't a mysterious object. It's a satellite that humans sent into space years ago. It just holds a bunch of songs from Earth.'

'Yes, yes!' Armstrong beamed. 'Armstrong was supposed to deploy the satellite into deep space, but Megavolt beamed Armstrong up before Armstrong could launch it.'

'You mean, this is just a music collection? There's no magical object that's going to give us musical superpowers?' Bash said slowly.

'It doesn't sound like it,' Neila groaned.

'But it *is* magical! It contains **EARTH'S GREATEST MUSIC**, sent out into the universe in the hope that it would be discovered by intelligent life!' Armstrong ran his fingers proudly along the box's smooth surface.

'Well, instead it's been rediscovered by a bunch of kids who are about to get their planet destroyed,' I said, giving the useless box a kick.

In my frustration, I kicked it a little harder than I meant to. It went spinning across the cargo bay and slammed into the wall with a **SMASH!** The satellite cracked and pieces of the pointless probe began to float around the rocket like space junk.

The four of us bobbed up and down in silence for a few minutes. Our quest to find awesome musical powers had failed.

'So that's it,' Bash said quietly.

And then I heard it.

A faint, familiar voice echoing around the cargo bay.

'What is that?' Neila asked.

'It's *music*. It's coming from the satellite,' Bash whispered, pointing at what was left of the little black box.

'That's not just any music.' I smiled. 'That's **MAX RIFF!**'

Between battling aliens and trying to save the world, I had totally forgotten about the other part of the *Minerva 7* story. The top-secret song recorded for the mission. The lost Max Riff and the Comets song that no one else in the world had ever heard . . .

UNTIL NOW!

Suddenly I understood what Megavolt had *meant* to beam up, instead of Armstrong.

The four of us floated in the cargo bay for the next three minutes without saying a word, just listening to the harmonics of the guitars, the deep vibrations of the drums, Max Riff's melodies. They all worked together to create this one perfect song. The music filled the cargo bay, surrounding us, flowing through us like some **MAGICAL ENERGY FORCE** that united us all together. Even though we were floating in zero gravity, it felt as if it was the music lifting us higher, changing us.

I guess this was that *perspiration* thing Max Riff was talking about, because when the song stopped I felt different. We all did.

'What just happened?' Neila whispered, her hands shaking a little.

'I don't know, but I think we were meant to discover this. We were supposed to find that song. It was our destiny,' I said.

'I feel . . . amazing. **UNSTOPPABLE!**' breathed Bash.

'Armstrong feels it too. Armstrong feels like anything is possible!'

As we looked into each other's eyes, I wondered if maybe we had discovered the power of **MUSICAL AWESOMENESS** after all. Maybe the power of musical awesomeness came from music itself.

And, if we had just listened to it, was it possible that the power was now inside us?

TRACK 28

BACK TO THE SPACE STADIUM

We raced back through the ghostly rocket to our stolen borrowed starship, dragging the pieces of the small black satellite with us. We listened to the lost Max Riff and the Comets song on repeat all the way back to the Space Stadium.

'Again!' Bash yelled as soon as it ended.

'AGAIN!' Neila ordered.

'AGAIN!' Armstrong screeched.

But the more we played this song, the more unstoppable we felt. It was as if the song was filling up my tank of awesomeness until it was overflowing, and I couldn't wait to get a guitar in my hands!

Armstrong twisted the starship through the asteroid field as we flew back to the docking space in the launch bay.

The stadium was busy now. Creatures had already started arriving for the final, and aliens from all over the galaxy were walking, crawling and floating down the hallways.

'Hey, look! Isn't that them?' a boggly-eyed creature screamed excitedly.

'It is! It's **THE EARTHLINGS!**' another cried.

'We're your biggest fans in the universe! Can we have your autograph?' they both said as they scuttled over to us.

'Er . . . sure,' I said, signing my name on their *I ♥ Earthlings* T-shirts.

Suddenly more of our fans arrived, trying to get our autographs and photos.

'Can I touch your fur?' one asked Armstrong as they stroked his head.

'Will you please sign my tentacles?' another said, holding out their sticky suckers.

Before long, we were totally surrounded. We could hardly move.

'Guys . . . I think we're famous!' Bash said.

'Yeah! What do we do now?' Neila asked.

'Run!' I yelled.

The four of us dived through the crowd, leading our fans on a chase through the backstage corridors. They were hot on our heels, tugging on our clothes, pulling at Armstrong's fur. One of them even managed to grab Neila's lucky hat!

'**NO!**' she screamed, throwing her hands on top of her head. 'My hat! I need it! It's my lucky hat!'

'Armstrong will get it!' Armstrong said, and he leaped into the air, swinging from the ceiling, and plucked the hat out of the fan-thief's hands with his awesome ape feet.

Security bots suddenly appeared and herded our new mega-fans away. '**ARTISTS ONLY. ARTISTS ONLY,**' the security bots droned, creating an uncrossable barrier that stopped the fans getting through. Armstrong swung back with the hat for Neila, and Neila quickly pulled it tightly over her hair.

'Thanks, Armstrong!' she breathed.

'What was all *that* about?' I said as we tumbled into our dressing room.

'Don't you get it? We're through to the final of the biggest show in the universe. Everyone in the cosmos will be tuning in to see us take on Megavolt. To see if we have what it takes,' Neila said.

'To see if we can win this battle!' Bash added.

'Can the worst band in the world become the best band in the universe?' I said.

The door suddenly swished open behind us.

'Beep-bop! **IT'S SHOWTIME!**' Beep-Bop bleeped.

The walk felt longer this time, as if we were moving in slow motion. This wasn't like the other battles. This one felt bigger. It felt epic. Every battle we'd played so far had brought us here, but so had every bad practice, every broken string. It all came down to this moment.

The alien crew lined the corridors and cheered us on and, as we approached the stage, the roadies stepped forward to hand us our guitars.

It was time for our pre-show checks. We zipped up our flight suits and adjusted our glittery mission patches. I cleaned my glasses. Neila pulled her lucky hat on tighter, and Bash brushed Armstrong's hair into a cool mohawk.

We were ready to rock.

The cheering crowd sounded like waves crashing against the shore as we stood at the side of the stage and watched Quark Blisterbum step into the stadium.

'Creatures of the universe, welcome to the **FINAL!**' he boomed, and the crowd went wild.

'You've witnessed pink furry aliens fluff it, squidliens have their hopes squashed, and rusty robots crumble under the pressure.'

As Quark spoke, the back of the stage disappeared to reveal all the cages from Megavolt's House of Boos, stacked right up to the vast, open stadium roof. Nebulas and swirling galaxies looked down at all the defeated bands trapped inside, forced to watch this final battle. Everyone was there. Dave and The Pincers; Dark Matter; even Annavoig and Mot, who were waving and giving us a thumbs-up.

'But tonight you shall witness the battle of all battles, as our finalists decided to Gravity Gamble and take on the unstoppable, unbeatable, totally unstable . . . **MEGAVOLT!**' Quark screamed.

The lights went out and the stadium was drenched in darkness.

'Can you feel that?' Bash asked as the stage started to rumble and the crowd began chanting: **'MEGAVOLT! MEGAVOLT! MEGAVOLT!'**

A white-hot plasma fist burst through the centre of the stage followed by another – **BOOM!**

Megavolt emerged from below, glowing with heat, power and fury.

'And, taking on the intergalactic rock legend . . . The Earthlings!' Quark announced.

We stepped out on to the stage, and I just knew we must look tiny compared to Megavolt.

'**MEGAVOLT HUNGRY.**' The titan-like star drooled, smiling at us as if he'd already won. '**BRING IN THE ROCK-o-METER!**' Megavolt demanded, and the huge device floated down.

'All right, folks, this is it. Whoever gets the rock-o-meter to hit **OUT OF THIS WORLD!** first **WINS!** Battling first, for the survival of Planet Earth, it's . . . **THE EARTHLINGS!**'

I called everyone in for a last-minute band meeting at the drum kit.

'OK, this is our shot. It's all or nothing. Either we're all going home or

none of us are,' I said as we huddled together.

'So, what song are we going to play?' Neila asked.

'"The Greatest Band in the Universe"?' suggested Bash.

'Ooh, ooh, or the one about Armstrong?' Armstrong said.

I thought about it for a moment, but none of those songs felt right.

'No. Let's play something **BRAND NEW!**' I grinned.

'Are you kidding? A new song? In the *final*?' Bash choked.

'Exactly! We can't just keep playing the same material. We need something new. Something fresh. Something . . . unplanned.' With that, I turned up the volume on my trusty Cosmo and started chugging a booming rhythm on the E-string.

DUM-DUM-BA-DUM-DUM-DUM-DUM-BA-DUM-DUM!

'What are you doing? We don't even know what you're playing!' Neila shrieked.

'Neither do I,' I said as the crowd started to clap

along to my thumping bass riff. **'I'M IMPROVISING.'**

'He's either gone totally bananas or he's a genius!' Bash said, looking at the thousands of clapping aliens in the audience.

'Did someone say bananas?' Armstrong chirped.

'Remember how we felt when we were listening to that lost Max Riff song? The power of music is inside us. We've just got to feel it,' I said to my band, and they all nodded.

Armstrong pulled out a set of drumsticks and handed them to Bash, while Neila watched what notes my fingers were playing.

'All right, I think I've got it,' she said as we turned to face our audience.

This was it. This was our moment. I gave Bash the nod and, with Armstrong on his back, the two of them took a deep breath and counted us in.

'ONE! TWO! THREE! FOUR!'

they shouted, and I started to sing.

SPACE BAND

by the Earthlings

Didn't believe in aliens
Until I saw some.
Getting beamed up into space
Was pretty awesome!
Let's rewrite history,
Forget all that you know.
We're not just kids from Earth,
So welcome to the show.

We are the Space Band! (Space Band!)
Rocking through the stars.
Light years across the universe,
A million miles from Mars.

We are the Space Band! (Space Band!)
Touring the unknown.
We don't need a star map
Cos the music guides us.

We couldn't play well.
We were far from the best.
We never gave up
And passed every rock-'n'-roll test.
So clear your minds because
We're coming into land.
We are not alone,
I finally understand.

We are the Space Band! (Space Band!)
Rocking through the stars.
Light years across the universe,
A million miles from Mars.

We are the Space Band! (Space Band!)
Touring the unknown,
We don't need a star map
Cos the music guides us home.

Did you ever wonder?
Wonder what it's like?
If we work together
And save the world tonight?

Let's rewrite history,
Forget all that you know.
We're not just kids from Earth,
So welcome to the show!
Welcome to the show!

We are the Space Band! (Space Band!)
Rocking through the stars.
Light years across the universe,
A million miles from Mars.

We are the Space Band! (Space Band!)
Touring the unknown,
And we'll be here forever
Like galaxy defenders.
We're the Space Band! (Space Band!)
And the music . . . (And the music!)
Yeah, the music guides us home!

The audience began cheering, raising the level on the rock-o-meter. For the first time ever, I felt my fingers going exactly where I wanted them to go on my bass without having to look down. It was as if they had a mind of their own, being controlled by an invisible force.

And it wasn't just my fingers. With four arms on the drums, Bash and Armstrong's double fills were rocking faster than ever, and Neila had found a way to make that dreaded school guitar absolutely sing. She wasn't hiding behind her fringe like usual, either. She was swinging her head around, head-banging like a guitar legend.

We were actually rocking!

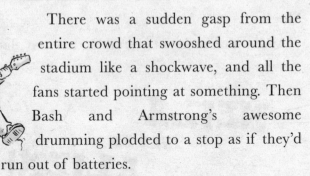

We are the Space Band! (Space Band!)
Rocking through the stars.
Light years across the universe,
A million miles from Mars.

We are the Space Band!
(Space Band!)
Touring the unknown,
We don't need a star map
Cos the music guides us home.

There was a sudden gasp from the entire crowd that swooshed around the stadium like a shockwave, and all the fans started pointing at something. Then Bash and Armstrong's awesome drumming plodded to a stop as if they'd run out of batteries.

'What are you doing?' I cried. 'Keep playing!'

But Bash's mouth was gawping open and his eyes were nearly popping out of his head. I followed his gaze to find the reason everyone was behaving so weirdly.

It was Neila.

She was still rocking out, slaying a sick riff on the guitar, banging her head forward and back and having the time of her life.

That was the problem. She must have headbanged so hard that she'd rocked her lucky hat right off her head – and it had revealed something unbelievable.

Something out of this world.

Something poking out of the top of her head . . .

It was an *antenna*!

Just one. Exactly like the ones that Annavoig and Mot had.

And in that moment everything fell into place.

NEILA WAS AN ALIEN!

TRACK 29

NEILA'S SECRET!

'STOP! STOP! STOP!' Megavolt exploded in anger, causing solar flares to erupt from his mouth.

Neila snapped out of her guitar solo and realized the whole stadium was watching her in silence. Then she spotted her lucky hat lying on the stage.

She turned to face me and Bash, and we just stared at her.

'So . . . I guess my secret isn't a secret any more,' she said.

'You're . . . you're an . . .' Bash stuttered in disbelief.

'An alien.' Neila bowed her head. Even her little antenna seemed to droop.

'How is that possible?!' I asked.

I guess the best sci-fi stories really do come in trilogies, because what Neila told us next made for the perfect final instalment of . . .

ROCKSTAR WARS: VOL. 3

In a distant world and a distant time, on the Planet Tenalp, a young alien watched her mum and dad's band battle against the almighty MEGAVOLT.

The band were . . . AWFUL. Worse than awful. They sucked harder than a vacuum cleaner. 'You're not going to make it!' the young alien screamed at the TV. But, before Megavolt could ZAP Planet Tenalp and eat it, she climbed into an escape pod and blasted into space . . . JUST IN TIME!

She soared through space and crashed into a strange blue-and-green planet . . .

. . . where she used her superior intelligence to cleverly disguise her alien appearance . . .

ultimate disguise

. . . and blend in with the creatures of her new home, Planet Earth! But she made a promise to herself . . . 'One day I'm going to join a band and defeat Megavolt, once and for all.'

A little while later . . .

'Hey, want to be in a band?' 'OK!' Soon, disguised as an Earthling, she was beamed across the universe to try to do what her parents couldn't — defeat Megavolt! Will she succeed? TO BE CONTINUED . . .

'So that UFO I saw crash in the woods last year. You didn't find it – you were **INSIDE** it?' Bash said.

Neila nodded.

'And they're your parents?' I asked, nodding at Annavoig and Mot.

'Yep,' Neila said. 'That's Mum and Dad.'

Now I understood why Neila had never invited us home to meet her parents. Why they had never shown up at the Christmas play or parents' evening. I also understood why Neila was so ridiculously, out-of-this-world clever. Why she liked broccoli, not chocolate. And why she had **NEVER ONCE** taken off her lucky hat!

Neila had once let slip that her mum and dad were musicians, I remembered. She'd just never said they were musicians from **ANOTHER PLANET** . . .

'But why didn't you tell us?' I asked.

Neila sighed. 'Because I just wanted to fit in. To belong.'

'So we have an imposter among our finalists! An Earthling who isn't actually from Earth!' Quark said, and there were mutters and whispers from the audience. 'We all know what this means.'

There was a glimmer of excitement in his eyes.

'Automatic disqualification!' he boomed.

Megavolt began licking his lips, salivating at the thought of devouring an early meal.

'MEGAVOLT HUNGRY! MEGAVOLT NEED MORE MASS!' he roared, and the crowd started chanting:

'ECLIPSE! ECLIPSE! ECLIPSE!'

'I'm so sorry,' whispered Neila.

We had come so far and got so close – only to be disqualified! We *were* good enough to defeat Megavolt. I could *feel* it. It all just seemed so unfair.

Bash and I put our arms round Neila and hugged her.

'It's not your fault,' I told her.

'Let's take one last look at the planet they couldn't save. Planet Earth, here are your best bits!' Quark said.

On the screens around the stadium, the image of Planet Earth swirling in the distance reappeared.

Then close-up images of our planet began to appear.

'What a peculiar little planet!' said Quark. 'Sitting on the edge of the Milky Way galaxy, home to billions of creatures of all sorts of weird shapes and sizes . . .'

As he spoke, the montage of images began to shift from busy, colourful city streets . . .

. . . to the snowy peaks of mountains . . .

. . . to impossibly tall skyscrapers . . .

. . . to giant redwood trees . . .

The alien audience was pointing in amazement. These places must have seemed so strange to them. We glimpsed whales, octopuses and seahorses under our oceans, then wild horses galloping across an open beach. Next came chimpanzees swinging through treetops (that brought tears to Armstrong's eyes), then streets and houses, families, kids in a playground . . . *home*.

'What a *confused* planet!' Quark chuckled. 'Oceans, deserts, cities, and so many different creatures! It's like Earth couldn't make up its mind!'

'**ENOUGH!**' Megavolt roared. He raised his burning fist, ready to smash it down on his big, dramatic red button and sentence our planet to his delicious destruction.

I suddenly thought about what Quark had said.

Confused?

Megavolt's fist came swooshing down.

So many different creatures . . .

'WAIT!' I blurted out, just before Megavolt's fist hit the button.

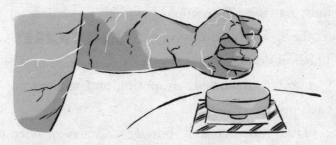

Everything paused.

The stadium was silent.

All eyes were on me, standing at the feet of the mighty Megavolt, who held the fate of our planet in his hands.

'You're right. Earth is a *confused* planet,' I agreed.

'What are you doing?' Neila hissed at me.

'Saving the world!' I whispered back.

I took a breath and faced the crowd.

'Earth has water and sand and mud and buildings and . . . all sorts of weird creatures that live in all of them,' I said. 'Being an Earthling isn't about looking a certain way or coming from a certain place. Just look at a goldfish and a giraffe,' I said, pointing to the images of Earth creatures on the huge stadium screens. 'They couldn't be more different, but they're both *Earthlings*. You could have skin or scales, fur or feathers. You could even have **ANTENNAE!** On Earth, it doesn't matter.'

The crowd started whispering and murmuring to each other.

'That's all very well, but *she* wasn't even born on your planet. That means she can't be an Earthling. **DISQUALIFIED!**' Quark snapped.

'You're right. She wasn't born on Earth,' I said. 'But it's her home now.'

There was a little rumble of applause from the audience.

'But . . . but . . . that doesn't *make* her an Earthling,' Quark said, laughing nervously.

'Well. Megavolt made Neila an Earthling when he destroyed her planet,' I said. 'But luckily for Neila – and for us – she crashed on the one planet where no one looks the same. A planet that doesn't just accept difference . . . we *celebrate* difference! That's why the sunshine and the rain don't cancel each other out. Together, they make rainbows!' I added, as a brilliant Earth-rainbow was projected across the stadium.

'So, for as long as Neila wants to call Earth her home, she *is* an Earthling, and that's why she belongs in this band.'

The crowd started a new chant:

'EARTHLINGS! EARTHLINGS!
EARTHLINGS!'

For the first time, Quark was lost for words. He looked at Megavolt, who was flaring with cosmic anger.

'Very well,' Megavolt conceded, and the audience erupted with applause.

WE STILL HAD A SHOT!

'I don't believe it, folks. The show isn't over yet!' Quark announced as we huddled around Bash's drum kit for a quick band meeting . . .

All except Neila.

She was still standing centre stage, facing the towering laser-beam cages holding the defeated bands – and, of course, her parents.

'If *I* can be an Earthling, then *they* can too!' Neila said.

'WHAT?!' Megavolt roared.

'You eclipsed all their planets and soon you'll destroy them, just like mine. So if Earth can be my new home, it can be theirs too,' Neila said – and I suddenly realized she was right.

I went and stood by her side.

'They might not look like us, or talk like us . . .'

'Or smell like us!' added Bash as a cloud of green trailed from the Gassy Giants.

'. . . but where we're from, when someone's in trouble and needs a place to call home, we put differences aside,' I explained.

'That's what it means to be an Earthling,' said Bash.

'It doesn't matter what you look like,' added Armstrong.

'Home isn't where you're *from* . . .' I smiled.

'It's where you **BELONG**,' Neila finished.

Quark's mouth fell open in shock. The whole stadium seemed to be buzzing with excitement. The entire universe was watching this moment.

'As representatives of Planet Earth, I officially invite all planetless aliens to become honorary *Earthlings*!' I cried.

There was silence as the universe seemed to hold its breath, waiting for Megavolt's response.

'SO BE IT,' he growled, glowing with anger from deep within his core.

The laser beams deactivated, releasing all the bands from their cages. The Pincers took up their instruments. Star Girl tuned up her awesome guitar and threw me her cosmic-green star-shaped glasses with a wink. The Big Bangs swung their beaters, and Neila's mum and dad got into position as this collection of cosmic creatures took their places by our side, creating one huge ultimate supergroup from the furthest reaches of the universe.

A SPACE BAND!

Megavolt's mouth curled into a hungry, evil snarl.

'Let them battle,' he roared.

'But . . . but . . . a **SUPERGROUP?** This has never happened before,' Quark stuttered nervously.

But Megavolt was too full of fiery fury now. **'LET'S ROCK!'** he boomed, swiping Quark Blisterbum off the stage.

The furious creature reached out with his glowing arms, stretched his fiery fingers wide and used the power of his gravitational pull to summon pieces of metal from the stage to his hands. He forged them together to assemble a mighty instrument of rock destruction – a guitar like I'd never seen before.

TRACK 30

ONE GIANT LEAP

The rock-o-meter powered back up and Megavolt wasted no time.

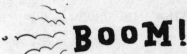

BOOM!

There was a blinding explosion of golden stars on the stage when he ripped into a face-melting guitar solo. The strings were literally on fire as he tapped scales I'd never even heard before, and the enormous stadium speakers could barely handle the noise.

The colossal creature thrashed around the stage, nailing knee slides that left a trail of burning embers behind him.

The rock-o-meter level instantly shot up from **BOOOO** to **ROCKTASTIC** and the stadium went wild.

'So, fellow Earthlings,' Dave said with a wink, 'what song are we playing?'

'And how are we all going to play together?' asked one of the Squid Sisters.

'Have you got the lyrics written out?' enquired Michael Doublé.

'What are the chords, man?' Star Girl asked.

'Oh no,' I said, suddenly realizing that I hadn't thought this through. 'Without time for a rehearsal, how will anyone know what to play?'

'Leave that to me,' Neila said with a smile.

She placed her hands on the side of her head, and her eyes and alien antenna began to glow a hypnotic green.

'Your powers!' Bash cheered, as suddenly **ALL** our new bandmates' eyes started to glow the same colour, as though they were syncing up to Neila's signal.

Neila raised her hand in the air, ready to rock a

power chord, and all the guitarists followed in perfect unison.

Bash and Armstrong rolled up the sleeves of their flight suits and counted us in at the exact same time as all the other drummers.

'**ONE! TWO! THREE! FOUR!**' they all cried – and our new supergroup burst into song, stealing the show from Megavolt. Spotlights swung over to us as I stepped up to the mic.

'Hello, Space Stadium!' I boomed, and the crowd replied with a mighty cheer. 'We're all the way from Planet Earth and we're here to rock your alien socks off!'

The crowd screamed as I started to sing . . .

We might look strange, but it's called diverse!
We've got superpowers so we don't rehearse.
Skip straight to the chorus – we don't need
    the verse . . .
We're the greatest space band in the universe!

Megavolt started glowing with fury, his hollow eyes smouldering from the anger deep within his core as the dial on the rock-o-meter began rising . . . and rising . . . and rising . . .

It shot straight past **ROCKTASTIC** and hit **SUPERSTARS!**

'**No!**' Megavolt roared.

But it was too late. We were on a roll. A rock 'n' roll!

Neila waved her hand like a conductor, and Star Girl stepped up to take centre stage. She cranked up the volume, and as Neila's fingers moved on that dreaded school guitar, Star Girl copied her melody. Together they shredded those strings so fast that it put Megavolt to shame.

Then Pixel Shift rearranged their pixels to create **THREE MORE** identical Star Girls, and together they played in awesome guitar harmony.

The Big Bangs followed Bash and Armstrong's beat, booming the stage with such force that it seemed to shake the whole stadium.

The Furry Wurzlets and The Pincers swapped

instruments, creating new, experimental sounds.

Michael Doublé combined with Slimeblob and Gloop to form the ultimate backing singers, as Neila projected the words directly into their minds.

'WE ARE THE GREATEST SPACE BAND IN THE UNIVERSE!' we all sang together as U.F.O. hovered their flying saucer over our heads, creating a laser show in time to the song. 8-TRAX scratched some rusty beats, while the Buxy brothers used their sugar-fuelled speed to spin Mini-Jack, the breakdancing bot, on his head.

As we all worked together, the rock-o-meter went soaring up the rock scale, stopping just under

OUT OF THIS WORLD!

We had almost won!

'I don't believe it!' cried Quark Blisterbum. 'The Earthlings are in the lead!'

'NO! I AM A STAR! NOBODY OUTSHINES ME!' Megavolt roared, creating a solar flare that sent a shockwave over the stage and across the stadium. The whole place rattled and shook as pieces of the stage started breaking apart, and the crowd dived for cover. Spotlights came loose and shot through the air towards Megavolt. He caught them in his burning jaws and swallowed them, getting bigger and brighter with each mouthful and glowing a brilliant red.

'What's happening to him?' I shouted.

'He's getting bigger!' Neila cried.

'Yeah, he's becoming a *red supergiant*!' Bash explained. 'This is fascinating –'

'This is no time for a science lesson, Bash! Just tell us what to do!' I shouted, as more and more chunks of stage and scenery flew into Megavolt's expanding mouth.

'I WILL BE THE BIGGEST STAR IN THE UNIVERSE!' Megavolt boomed as he smashed his own burning guitar in rock rampage and swallowed it whole, sending the rock-o-meter into overdrive.

Suddenly Megavolt swelled to such an enormous size that he cracked through the side of the Space Stadium, revealing the looming darkness of the black hole outside.

'Spectra! That's it!' said Bash as his drumsticks were pulled out of his hand by Megavolt's increasing gravity and flew into his mouth. 'Do you remember what happens to stars when they get too big?'

For the first time **EVER**, I did actually remember one of his nerdy space facts. 'They go supernova!' I yelled.

'Right! They explode!' He smiled like a proud teacher.

'So, to defeat Megavolt, we need to . . . make him a bigger star?'

Suddenly the force of his gravity started pulling everyone towards him. All the members of our new supergroup grabbed hold of anything they could to stop themselves from being sucked in! Megavolt was out of control and it wouldn't take much more to send him over the edge, to make him go supernova . . . but the dial on the rock-o-meter was going crazy for Megavolt's rock meltdown, and as his reading drew level with ours, the red button that was primed and ready to eclipse Earth started glowing.

'YOU SEE! IT'S ALL OVER FOR YOU PUNY EARTHLINGS!'

Megavolt bellowed.

'YOUR PATHETIC PLANET WAS ALWAYS MINE!'

He looked down at the flashing red button and raised his flaming fist ready to destroy our home.

This was it.

It was now or never.

I had to do something so undeniably *rock* that it would end this battle once and for all.

'**YOU WILL NEVER OUTSHINE ME!**' Megavolt boomed.

'**THAT'S IT!**' I yelled.

I realized that I needed to do the one thing I said I'd never do. The most rock 'n' roll thing in the universe.

I took off my cosmic-green Fender P. Bass, my Cosmo. I held the long neck in my hands.

'Thank you for everything!' I whispered.

Then I turned to Neila. 'Neila, I need a lift!' I shouted, and I ran towards Megavolt and took one giant leap into the air.

Neila placed her hands on the side of her head and I felt her power lift me towards the unstable star. Higher and higher over the stadium I soared, defying all the laws of physics, as I swung my bass guitar over my head like an axe, just like Max Riff did at the end of his concert.

'Hey, Megavolt! **EAT THIS!**' I cried, and he turned his glowing face just in time to see me perform the ultimate rock finishing move and smash my guitar . . . into his blazing mouth.

The moment it touched the surface of his flaming face, our reading on the rock-o-meter rocketed beyond **OUT OF THIS WORLD** – and off the charts. There was an explosion of galactic proportions and a blinding pulse of energy suddenly blasted across the stadium . . .

. . . and when the stardust settled, there was silence.

Megavolt was gone.

TRACK 31

HOME

The stadium was messier than my bedroom on Christmas morning. There were bits of instruments everywhere. Tangles of guitar strings poked out from under blown amps, cracked cymbals and broken drum skins. It was like a rock graveyard.

'Is everyone OK?' I called.

'I think so,' croaked Bash, climbing out of the debris.

'Yeah, I'm still in one piece,' said Neila, straightening her antenna.

'Armstrong here too!' said Armstrong, swinging down from above as the faces of our new space bandmates emerged from under the rock rubble. We dusted ourselves off and stood in what was left of the Space Stadium.

'LOOK!' Bash yelled, pointing up above where there was not one but *two* black holes, swirling darkly side by side.

Neila smiled. 'I guess he couldn't handle the stardom.'

Quark Blisterbum clambered out from underneath the wrecked rock-o-meter. 'Well, folks, it looks like we have a new champion. The **WINNERS** of the Intergalactic Battle of the Bands: *The Earthlings*!' Quark coughed before fainting in shock.

The audience, who were still climbing out from under their seats, went wild. Shooting stars started swirling across the galaxy in celebration, and everyone began chanting: '**EARTHLINGS! EARTHLINGS! EARTHLINGS!**'

'I guess we're not the worst band in the world any more!' Bash laughed.

I smiled. 'No, we're the best band in the universe!'

'What do we do now?' asked Neila, looking around. 'Where do we go?'

'Home,' I replied. 'We **ALL** go home. Look!'

Suddenly all the holograms of the eclipsed planets around the stadium came back to life – the purple (probably pee) oceans of the Squid Sisters' planet, the rusty-red desert surface of 8-TRAX and Mini-

Jack's home, the Furry Wurzlets' giant sphere of pink fluff – all of them alive and beaming with colour and life.

Dave smiled at us. 'They've been uneclipsed. You did it.'

'No, **WE** did it!' I replied.

Suddenly the blue rings of fizzing energy started to appear around us all, just as they had appeared on the day we were beamed up from Earth.

'This is it. We're going home!' Bash cheered.

'George, do you think my family will be welcome on Earth too?' Neila said nervously.

'Are you kidding? Your family just helped save the world! I can't wait to show it to them!' I grinned as the beams of blue circled Annavoig, Mot and their two band members too.

'Will we ever see you all again?' I said to our new alien friends. Everyone fell silent as they realized this was goodbye.

'I'm not sure. But next time you're looking up at the stars, you'll know that the sky is full of friends twinkling back at you,' said Dave.

'More than friends. **BANDMATES!**' I whooped, raising my fist in the air, throwing them all the rock sign.

'Rock on, Earthlings,' Dave said, raising his claw, followed by the members of Ozone, then Dark Matter, Star Girl and everyone else until there was a crowd of rock fists in the air.

'Rock on!' we replied joyfully as the blue energy engulfed us all.

'Hold on tight, Armstrong!' Bash said.

'**ARMSTRONG GOING HOME!**' Armstrong cheered as he excitedly zipped himself inside Bash's backpack.

There was a sudden fizz of electricity as our feet started levitating over the stage, and I grabbed my book of rock and made sure it was safely tucked inside my pocket. After one final wild roar from the crowd, we were all beamed up and out of the Space Stadium, whizzing our separate ways across the universe. We blasted away from the black hole that was now Megavolt, soared across star systems, glided over galaxies, crossed clusters of comets . . . until we were flying back through the Milky Way.

Our blue beams of pure, sparkling starlight energy steered well clear of Uranus, sailed round Saturn, and zoomed straight towards a tiny bluey-green dot in the distance.

'THAT'S IT!' I cried.

'Home!' bellowed Armstrong.

A few moments later, we were entering Earth's atmosphere, falling through fluffy clouds and heading straight for a familiar-looking square building below.

I smiled. 'I never thought I'd say this, but **I CAN'T WAIT** to get back to school!'

'Me too!' said Neila.

'Me three!' laughed Bash.

'Armstrong four!' added Armstrong.

In a flash of blazing blue, we beamed back through the roof of the school hall, where everyone was still frozen as though they were on pause. As our feet touched down on the stage, the blue energy started to **FIZZLE** out and the world around us began to come to life, as if it was defrosting.

'It's like we never left!' gasped Bash.

'Which means there's one battle left,' Neila said, pointing at Alfie Biffson and his band glaring at us.

'The Boneheadz!' we said together.

'Armstrong ready!' Armstrong said, pulling out a set of drumsticks, ready to play.

'Yeah, except I don't have a guitar . . .' I sighed, looking at my empty hands.

Suddenly there was a flicker of energy, like tiny atoms of stardust catching the light. Particles of cosmic-green started to reassemble in my hands and by the time the world had unfrozen I had my Fender P. Bass back, ready to **ROCK.**

'But I thought this was destroyed?' I said, running my fingers over the sparkling body.

'Don't you remember the rules?' Bash smiled. 'The winners are returned to their home planet, to the moment they left, just like . . .'

'. . . just like it never happened!' I grinned.

There was an abrupt gasp from the crowd of shocked students and concerned parents as reality kicked back in, and they stared at the chimpanzee dressed as an astronaut that had suddenly joined us on the school stage.

'Wow! Those are some pretty wild costumes! I didn't realize it was a fancy-dress competition,' Mr Biffson sneered.

'These aren't fancy-dress costumes. We're **ROCK STARS** and these are our stage outfits,' I said, zipping up my flight suit.

'I made those! That's my boy!' my mum shouted proudly from the back of the hall.

'Oh, you must be George's mum and dad! We're Neila's parents!' Annavoig said as she and Mot edged their way through the busy crowd.

'Lovely to meet you finally! Here, I've made you T-shirts!' Mum trilled, shoving her homemade world's-most-embarrassing T-shirts over Annavoig and Mot's heads.

'Well, *rock stars*, show us what you can do,' Mr Biffson said, holding his clipboard in his arms and raising one eyebrow.

'Bash, hit it!' I said, and Bash counted us in.

'ONE! TWO! THREE! FOUR!'

he screamed, and with the power of musical awesomeness inside us, we rocked that school like it had never been rocked before.

The crowd went wild. Even the teachers were

screaming for us and, as Neila ripped into a rocking guitar solo on the dreaded school guitar, I saw Alfie Biffson's mouth drop open like his face had been melted by rock awesomeness.

Those three minutes were the best three minutes of my life. We didn't care about winning, we weren't thinking about the prize, and we didn't need to save the world any more. We were just a band, rocking out, making people happy for three minutes. Because that's what music is all about.

As we finished the song, the rock-o-meter level soared up to the maximum score – **OUT OF THIS WORLD** – making us joint first place on the leader board with the Boneheadz.

'It's a tie!' announced Mr Biffson.

'Are you kidding? We just defeated the biggest rock star in the universe and we can't even beat the Boneheadz!' Neila huffed.

'As the rules clearly state, in the event of a tie, the winner shall be decided by the head judge. ME!' He grinned. 'So I can now reveal that the winner of the Battle of the Bands is . . . **THE BONEHEADZ!**'

'HA! You suck, *Earthlings*!' Alfie yelled as he ran on to the stage to claim his prize.

'Congratulations! We – I mean, *you* have won front-row tickets to the **SOLD-OUT** Max Riff and the Comets concert!' Mr Biffson cheered as he handed the tickets over to Alfie.

As the Boneheadz celebrated their victory, we stood at the back of the stage feeling as deflated as a balloon the day after a birthday party. Sure, we had saved the world, but seeing Max Riff and the Comets play would have been the icing on the cake. And now that cake was going to be eaten by Alfie Stinking Biffson.

Or was it . . .?

'Hold it!' called a wise, raspy voice from the shadows at the back of the school hall.

There was a sudden gasp from the parents, squeals of excitement from the teachers and confused whispers from the students as a mysterious figure stepped forward.

I knew who it was in a heartbeat.

There was only one person in the world who had

hair as wild as a lion, a leather jacket flung over his shoulder, arms covered in tattoos, and enormous dark sunglasses, even though he was indoors . . .

'**MAX RIFF!**' I whispered as the audience parted and the legend himself made his way to the stage.

(I KNOW!)

I couldn't believe what I was seeing. Was this real? Was this a dream? Was **THE** Max Riff actually here, in my school? If I hadn't just been beamed back from outer space, I would have said this was totally impossible – but just to be safe I dropped to my knees and bowed my head as if I was meeting the Queen of England. This was rock royalty, after all!

'Mr Riff? W-w-what are you doing here at Greyville School?' Mr Biffson stammered nervously.

'Me and the dudes were on our way to rehearse for the concert on Saturday night when I heard the sweet sound of rock blasting from this very hall, dude,' Max explained, his voice commanding silence like a magic spell. 'So we stopped the Comet bus to watch the gig and witnessed a rock miracle, dude. A band that was so *out-of-this-world* awesome that me and the dudes wanted to ask those dudes to be special guests and play at our concert on Saturday night . . . dude.'

'**YES!** Ha-ha! In your face, Earthlings!' Alfie gloated. 'Did you hear that? We're going to be **PLAYING** at the Max Riff show! We won't be needing *these* any more!' And he ripped up his concert tickets into tiny pieces, in front of my face.

'No, dude, not *you*,' Max Riff said. 'I'm talking about *those* dudes. **THE EARTHLINGS**.'

I looked up and saw Max Riff pointing right at me.

'You dudes rock so hard! We'd love The Earthlings to be our opening support act. What do you say?'

We could barely speak, but as Max Riff himself put his hand up to high-five me, I managed to nod my head.

'You know, little dudes,' he said, 'if you keep rocking like you just did, one day you might be the greatest band in the universe.'

And I didn't have the heart to tell him that we already were.

THE END

THIS BOOK HAS A SOUNDTRACK!
THE SONGS FROM

SPACE BAND

PERFORMED BY

ARE AVAILABLE NOW!

Just scan this QR code to listen:

https://linktr.ee/spacebandalbum
This will take you to another website,
so please ask a grown-up.

ACKNOWLEDGEMENTS

GROUND CONTROL, DO YOU READ ME?

This is Captain T. Fletcher here. I'm currently travelling at lightspeed through an uncharted region of the universe, beaming this special message across the galaxy to the many people who made this book possible. People whose talents are so mind-bogglingly out of this world that I'm pretty sure most of them are aliens disguised as humans, living among you all on Planet Earth.

The first 'people' I want to thank are my McFLY bandmates: Danny, Dougie and Harry. This book is largely inspired by our twenty-light-year journey across the galaxy as McFLY, and if it wasn't for you guys giving up your free time and awesome rock skills, then the *Space Band* album wouldn't have happened. Thanks, guys. I owe you.

Thanks to all the Galaxy Defenders who have been

following my band across the universe and supporting my writing journey. This one is yours.

Thanks to my intergalactically incredible editor – Natalie Doherty (100% alien!) – plus Wendy Shakespeare, India Chambers, Emily Smyth, Adam Webling, *inter*-Stella Newing and all the other extraterrestrials hiding among the editorial, design, production and audio teams at PRH.

ALERT! Watch out for these highly dangerous shape-shifters who have infiltrated the sales team: Kat Baker, Toni Budden, Rozzie Todd, Sophie Marsden, Autumn Evans, Becki Wells, Amy Wilkerson . . . And I'm picking up a reading that the invasion has spread to the rights team too: Alice Grigg, Maeve Banham, Susanne Evans, Beth Fennell and Anda Podaru. All are 100% non-human. Don't be deceived by their talents – approach with caution.

I've just been informed that the marketing and PR team have been beamed up by a UFO: Harriet Venn, Phoebe Williams, Lottie Halstead and Mhari Nimmo. I hope you're beamed back in time for my next book.

And finally, from Planet PRH, thanks to the beings that are to blame for all these books: Tom Weldon, Francesca Dow and Amanda Punter. They're far too nice to be from this planet. 100% aliens.

Thanks to Shane Devries and all at Dynamo who worked on the astronomically astounding illustrations for lighting up these pages with your starlight.

Thanks to my manager, Rachel Drake, for holding my whole world together. It would definitely fall apart without you! And thanks to my wonderful agent, Stephanie Thwaites, for always making sure my oxygen supplies are sufficient for my space travels (among other things).

Thanks to Chris Sheldon, Marek Deml, Matt Milton and all who worked at lightspeed to bring the *Space Band* album to Earth. What a team! I'm so proud of it.

To Mum and Dad for encouraging the two childhood interests that inspired this book: space and rock! And to my sister, Carrie, for being so annoyingly talented/inspiring.

Thanks to my wife, Giovanna, who has levels of

patience that just aren't found in human beings, and to my three aliens . . . sorry, *kids*, Buzz, Buddy and Max for being my biggest inspiration (and toughest critics!).

Finally, thanks to all the creatures, wherever you are from this universe, who read my books and listen to my music. I'm so, so lucky to have people enjoy what I make. It makes the long nights in hyper-sleep worth it.

CAPTAIN T. FLETCHER, OVER AND OUT.

HAVE YOU READ ALL OF
TOM FLETCHER'S
BRILLIANT STORIES?

It can be sad when
a story comes to an end.

So why stop reading
when you don't have to?

Let's dive into the world of...

...the Creakers

THE NIGHT IT ALL BEGAN

The sun disappeared behind the pointed silhouettes of the rooftops of Whiffington Town, like a hungry black dog swallowing a ball of flames.

A thick, eerie darkness fell like no other night Whiffington had ever known. The moon itself barely had enough courage to peek round the clouds, as though it knew that tonight something strange was going to happen.

Mothers and fathers throughout Whiffington tucked their children into bed, unaware that this would be the last bedtime story, the last goodnight kiss, the last time they'd switch off the light.

Midnight.

One o'clock.

Two o'clock.

Three o'clock.

CREAK . . .

A strange noise broke the silence.

It came from inside one of the houses. With the whole town fast asleep, who could possibly have made that sound?

Or perhaps not *who* but *WHAT*?

. . . CREAK!

There it was again. This time from another house.

Creak!

Creeaak!

CREEEAAAAAK!

THE NIGHT IT ALL BEGAN

The sound of creaky wooden floorboards echoed around the hallways of every home in Whiffington.

Something was inside.

Something was creaking about.

Something not human.

There were no screams. There were no nightmares. The children slept peacefully, wonderfully unaware that the world around them had changed. It had all happened silently, as if by some strange sort of dark magic, and they wouldn't know anything about it until they woke up the next morning, on the day it all began . . .

CHAPTER ONE
THE DAY IT ALL BEGAN

L*et's start on the day it all began.*

On the day it all began, Lucy Dungston woke up.

Right. Well, that's a start, but it's not very exciting, is it? Let's try again.

On the day it all began, Lucy Dungston woke up to a rather unusual sound . . .

OK, that's a little better. Let's see what happens next . . .

It was the sound of the alarm clock ringing in her mum's bedroom.

Well, it's got a bit boring again, hasn't it? Let's try that bit one more time . . .

THE DAY IT ALL BEGAN

It was the sound of the alarm clock ringing in her mum's bedroom because Lucy's mum wasn't there to switch it off. You see, Lucy was about to find out that while she was asleep in the night her mum had disappeared . . .

OH. MY. GOSH!

Imagine waking up to find that your mum had disappeared in the night! It gives me the creepy tingles every time I tell this story. I bet you're thinking, This is going to be the best scary story ever. I can't wait to read it and tell all my friends that I'm really brave because I wasn't even one bit scared.

Even though you were totally scared all the way through.

Well, this is only just the beginning. Wait until you read what happens later when the Creakers come out.

Let me know if you get scared . . . because I am!

Back on the day it all began, Lucy climbed out of bed, slipped on her fluffy blue dressing-gown and walked across her creaky floorboards, which were warm from the morning sunlight creeping in through the curtains.

Would you like to know what Lucy looked like?

Of course you would! Here's a picture . . .

As you can see, she had shorter hair than most girls, and it was as brown as mud, or chocolate, and even though Lucy liked it to be short, her mum insisted she keep a fringe.

'It stops you looking like a boy!' her mum would say (this was before she disappeared, of course). This really wound Lucy up, as her fringe always seemed to flop into her eyes, meaning she constantly had to lick her hand and slick it over to one side just so she could see.

Her eyes, once the fringe was out of the way, were greeny-brown . . . or perhaps browny-green. Either way, they were a bit green and a bit brown. You could say there was nothing particularly remarkable about Lucy at all, and it's true; she was no different from any other child in Whiffington, which is another way of saying she was quite remarkable indeed.

Anyway, more about that later.

'Mum?' Lucy called, padding across the landing towards her mum's bedroom.

But of course you already know there was no reply because her mum was gone!

Lucy's heart started beating faster in her chest as she gently opened the bedroom door and stuck her head inside.

Mrs Dungston's book was still on the bedside table, a bookmark poking out, with her reading glasses perched on top. Her empty cocoa cup with the yellow polka-dot pattern sat beside it. Her slippers were neatly positioned on the floor. It was all as it usually was. Except for the piercing ringing of the alarm clock and the spooky, empty bed.

Lucy stopped the alarm clock and ran to check the bathroom.

Empty bath.

Empty shower.

Empty loo (although Lucy would have been very surprised to find her mum hiding in there).

She ran downstairs.

Empty kitchen.

Empty living room.

Empty everywhere.

'Mum? **MUM?**' she called, a note of panic rising in her voice, and her heart leaping like a frog in her chest.

She was beginning to get an awful feeling that something terrible might have happened . . . and it was a feeling that Lucy already knew.

You see, the really creepy thing was that this wasn't the first time it had happened to Lucy Dungston.

A few months ago her dad had vanished too!

Unbelievable, right?

Lucy's mum had been devastated.

'Must have run off with another woman,' Lucy had

heard one of the other mums whispering in the school playground.

'What a cheating, rotten man!' another had said, shaking her head.

But Lucy didn't think her dad was rotten at all. She couldn't believe he would run off without saying goodbye to her, without leaving a note, without saying where he was going, without finishing the half-eaten chocolate Hobnob and barely sipped cup of tea she'd found on his bedside table the next morning.

So on *this* morning, on the day it all began, Lucy had the strangest feeling that somehow this was all connected, that something weird was going on.

Lucy ran down the hallway, snatched the phone from the little wobbly table and dialled her mum's mobile number (which she knew off by heart for emergencies, like every sensible eleven-year-old should). But, as her mum's phone started ringing, Lucy saw it flashing on the arm of the sofa.

Lucy ended the call and hung her head in defeat.

Defeat . . . feet . . . shoes . . . her mum's shoes!

She ran to the front door. A pair of cosy, flat slip-ons

with flower-shaped sparkly bits were sitting on the mat, exactly where her mum kicked them off every night and where she'd slip back into them before leaving the house each day. Surely her mum wouldn't have left the house without her shoes . . . would she?

Lucy's heart sank. This all seemed far too familiar. On the day her father disappeared, one of the strangest things was that his favourite chunky black boots with the yellow laces, which he wore every single day, were still sitting by the front door, like he'd never left. Just like her mum's shoes!

Lucy knew there was only one thing for it. She was going to have to call the police.

She'd never done that before, and her heart was pounding like a drum in her chest as she pressed the number nine three times with a shaky, nervous finger.

Now what do you suppose happened next? If you think a police officer answered the phone and said, '*It's OK, Lucy, we've found your mum and we'll bring her home right away and we'll even pick up some breakfast for you too. What would you like?*' then you'd be very wrong indeed and should probably never write a book.

What actually happened was possibly the worst thing Lucy could think of . . .

Nothing.

The phone just rang, and rang, and rang, and carried on ringing until Lucy hung up.

'Since when do the police not answer the phone?' Lucy said to herself, her voice sounding unusually loud in the empty house.

A little voice in her head told her the answer: *When something spooky is going on . . .*

Lucy pulled open the front door and stepped out into the stinking morning air. Oh, it was quite normal for the air to be stinky outside the Dungston family's house. It smelled like a mixture of bum gas with a hint of mature sock cheese, and had a sharp after-scent of freshly brewed cabbage. It wasn't the house that smelled – it was the truck parked in the driveway. It was one of those chunky, clunky, nostril-stinging, rubbish-collecting trucks that trundle around town with those jolly-looking, grubby people in grimy overalls collecting everyone's rotten rubbish bags.

Lucy's dad had been one of those jolly-looking,

grubby rubbish-collecting people. He was the bin man for Whiffington Town, where he lived – *sorry*, where he USED to live – before he disappeared. Since he vanished, his truck had been parked in the driveway, stinking out the whole street. Of course, Mrs Dungston had tried to sell the truck, but no one wanted a stinky old thing like that. Even Whiffington Scrap Metal said that the pong was too strong for them to crush it! And so there it stayed, on Lucy's driveway.

If you ever find yourself behind one of these trucks, take a little sniff, just a little one, and you'll know what Lucy Dungston's house smelled like.

Anyway, back to the day it all began!

Out in Lucy's street, Clutter Avenue, she noticed instantly that things weren't right. Usually there was a long line of traffic clogging up the road as mums and dads took their kids to school and went to work and drove to the post office and the hairdresser's and did all the boring stuff grown-ups do. But today the road wasn't busy. It wasn't just not-busy – it was completely deserted. Not a single car. Lucy looked left, then right, then left again, then right again, then she repeated that about twenty more times, which I won't bother to write because that would just be silly, but when she had finished she was convinced she was right – something weird was definitely happening in Whiffington Town.

'What the jiggins is going on?' she said to herself.

What the jiggins indeed, Lucy.

Where was Mr Ratcliffe, the wrinkly old man who did yoga in his front garden in his underpants? (He claimed it was the secret to staying young.)

Where was Molly the milk lady, who delivered fresh bottles of milk from her electric van?

Where was Mario, the Italian man from the next street, who jogged past every morning in his skimpy Lycra shorts?

Where *was* everyone?!

That's when Lucy heard a noise. Her heart leapt. Was it her mum?

A long, slow creak came from somewhere along Clutter Avenue, followed by a sudden **CLANG!**

'Hello?' Lucy called.

'Mama?' a small voice asked from behind the garden fence two doors down.

'Oh, Ella! It's just you!'

Lucy sighed in relief as Ella Noying appeared. First her bouncy Afro hair peeped out into the street, followed by her round cheeks and her big deep brown eyes that always managed to get her out of trouble. She was wearing bright pink pyjamas made of shiny silk, with her initials embroidered on the pocket. In one hand was a pair of pink, heart-shaped designer sunglasses. Lucy never saw Ella anywhere without those.

'Lucy, I can't find Mama or Papa and my avocado needs mashing,' Ella whined.

Before Lucy could reply, another door opened across the street.

'Dad?' whispered Norman Quirk, a boy from Lucy's year at school, as he hesitantly stepped into his front garden. Norman was dressed in a pristinely ironed, meticulously clean Scout uniform, which was covered in the most achievement badges Lucy had ever seen.

Here is a list of some of Norman's badges:

- a *tree-climbing* badge
- a *tent-pitching* badge
- a badge for *spreading-butter-on-toast-all-the-way-to-the-edges*
- the *indoor-challenge* badge
- the *outdoor-challenge* badge
- the *shake-it-all-about-door challenge* badge
- a *bed-making* badge
- a *cake-baking* badge
- an *eating-the-cake-you-bake-in-the-bed-you-make* badge
- the *remembering-to-wash-your-belly-button* badge
- and even a badge for *collecting-lots-of-badges*

. . . and there were a few empty spots on his uniform he needed to fill with new badges.

'Oh, hi . . . Er, I mean, good morning, civilians!'

Norman said, nervously holding up three fingers in Scout salute, before fiddling with his neatly combed, mousy-blond hair. With his other hand, he covered his mouth to hide his train-track braces.

'You haven't seen my dad, have you?' he asked, scooping a handful of mud from his front garden and sniffing it as if trying to pick up his dad's scent. When Norman bent down, Lucy caught sight of his Transformers socks.

Ella giggled at him, not really in a mean way, but just because she found Norman sort of funny. Everyone did. Norman was . . . different.

Sometimes people who are different get laughed at, but it's always the different ones who make a difference, Lucy heard her dad's voice say in her head. He had his own way of looking at things. On cloudy days, he'd tell Lucy, 'The sun just needs a holiday so it can shine better tomorrow!' When she came second to her friend Giorgina in the sack race on Sports Day, he told her, 'Don't be upset. You just made your friend really happy!' And, when she asked him if he liked being a bin man, he said, 'You'd be surprised what people throw away, Lucy. One man's rubbish is another man's favourite pair of black boots!' and clipped his heels together with a wink.

'No, I've not seen your dad, sorry,' Lucy said, shaking off her daydream about her own father and elbowing Ella to stop her laughing. 'My mum's missing too.'

Suddenly another door opened and Sissy McNab ran out into the street in tears. Then Toby Cobblesmith, who had his shoes on the wrong feet. Next out came William Trundle and Brenda Payne, searching for their mum and dad, then another kid, and another, until, one by one, every child in Whiffington Town came stumbling out of their houses in their PJs, dressing-gowns and slippers, trying to find their parents. Nans and grandads, aunts and uncles – they were all gone too. There wasn't a single grown-up to be seen.

There was such a kerfuffle in Clutter Avenue: some children were crying; others were laughing; and a few were still fast asleep in bed and hadn't noticed anything yet.

'What's going on?' they shouted (the ones who were awake).

'Where are our parents?' they called.

'What are we going to do?' they yelled.

Lucy took a breath and tried to think. 'What would my mum do?' she said to herself. 'How did my mum find out what was going on in the world?'

Then, before she knew what she was doing, Lucy found herself clambering on to the steps of her dad's stinking rubbish truck, and above the noise she yelled . . .

'THE NEWS!'

There was silence. Everyone turned to look at Lucy.

'We have to watch the news! I know it's super-boring, but whenever my mum wants to know what's going on in the world she always watches the news,' she told them.

The children looked at each other, uncertain. I'm sure you know that the news is the biggest snorefest on TV, but Lucy had a point.

'She's right . . .' Norman whispered to Ella, too frightened to say it out loud.

'SHE'S RIGHT!' Ella shouted, not frightened of anyone.

'To the television!' they all cried in unison, and every

THE DAY IT ALL BEGAN

child on Clutter Avenue in Whiffington Town pushed past Lucy and piled into her house.

In a matter of seconds her living room was full from carpet to ceiling with scared children in their PJs. There were children sitting on the floor. There were children sitting on the children sitting on the floor.

There were even children sitting on the children sitting on the children sitting on the floor! They were all terrified, mainly because their parents were missing, but also a little bit freaked out because they were about to watch the news without being made to.

Lucy switched on her TV.

'Have you got any popcorn?' asked a child sitting on the floor.

'Sorry, I don't think we do,' Lucy replied.

'Chocolate Hobnobs?' asked a child sitting on the child sitting on the floor.

'No chocolate Hobnobs either. Mum doesn't buy those any more. Not since – well, never mind. We just don't have any.'

'You mean we have to watch TV without any snacks?' moaned Ella, who was sitting on the child sitting on the child sitting on the floor.

'Oh, OK – I'll see what we've got!' promised Lucy, whizzing off to the kitchen. She returned a few minutes later with all the boxes of cereal from the cupboard and handed them around the room. 'Take a handful and pass it on,' she said, then got back to finding the twenty-four-hour news channel.

The moment it flicked on, her heart stopped.

'Oh no!' Lucy cried. **'Look!'**

The crowd of children all spat out their cornflakes and Cheerios in shock, showering the room with chewed bits of soggy cereal.

On the TV they could see the normal news desk, the normal sheets of paper and the normal coffee mug, but there was something very *not*-normal about it.

The news presenter was missing!

Ella pushed through to the front. 'Try another channel! Maybe your TV is broken, Lucy. Don't you have a *TV-repair* badge?' she demanded, turning to Norman, who tried his best to hide when everyone looked at him.

'Perhaps I could take a look?' he said sheepishly as the children nudged him across the room towards the telly. 'Sorry, oops, watch out!' he muttered as he stepped on almost everybody's fingers.

'Well? Why isn't it working?' Ella said, bashing the remote on the side of the TV.

'Erm . . . well . . . I actually *do* have a badge in *TV-remote-control functions*. And as the only member of the Whiffington Scout Troop present today –'

'Aren't you the *only* member of the Scout Troop, full stop?' asked Ella. Everybody laughed.

Norman sat down, looking defeated, on what he thought was the arm of the sofa, but it was actually the head of another child sitting on another child.

'Here, just do your best,' Lucy said, taking the remote from Ella and handing it to Norman. Norman smiled at her, for once forgetting to hide his braces. He flicked through a few channels, hoping to find a grown-up of any kind looking back out at them.

Silly Sunrise, the kids' show, had no Funzo the Clown getting pied in the face today. *Wakey-Wakey, Whiffington* had no Piers Snoregan, although that was probably an improvement. Norman flicked through the sports channels, the shopping network, the cooking shows, Whiffington Weather and just about every channel he could think of. Not a single one of them had a single grown-up.

THE DAY IT ALL BEGAN

It was almost as if every adult on the planet had just disappeared overnight, from Lucy's mum to the news presenter . . .

. . . they had all just **GONE!**